The Merchant & Marina

SUMMER ROSE
PECK

Copyright © 2022 by Summer Rose Peck

All rights reserved. No part of this book may be reproduced in any form by electronic or mechanical means, including information storage and retrieval systems, without permission in writing from the publisher, except by a reviewer who may quote brief passages in a review.

This is a work of fiction. Names, characters, places, and incidents are either products of the author's imagination or are used fictitiously. Any resemblance to actual persons, living or dead, or locales is entirely coincidental.

THE MERCHANT
& MARINA

CONTENTS

CHAPTER ONE
THE EXODUS

CHAPTER TWO
THE BOATHOUSE

CHAPTER THREE
THE SURVIVOR

CHAPTER FOUR
THE MERMAID

CHAPTER FIVE
THE WHALERMAN

CHAPTER SIX
THE HUNT

CONTENTS

CHAPTER SEVEN
THE TAVERN

CHAPTER EIGHT
THE SURRENDER

CHAPTER NINE
THE ANGEL

CHAPTER TEN
THE GALLEON

CHAPTER ELEVEN
THE SUNSET

CHAPTER TWELVE
THE FINALE

*"Even a captain at his helm can be thrown off course
when met by opposing squalls."*

- *Summer Rose Peck*

CHAPTER ONE

THE EXODUS

In the year of our Lord, eighteen hundred and forty, the American cargo ship *Exodus* rolled swiftly across rough North Atlantic seas. She crested every swell, furiously, and when the bow sank forward into the deep, every honest seaman would pray for her to mount the next wave and the next just as mercifully as the last.

Bearing dead on into a squall, this vessel had been readily prepared for the heavy sou'wester beyond the bowsprit. Her sheets were checked, and many hands stowed themselves deep in her bowels till the morrow. Oncoming swells shroud every crevice on *Exodus* with sea water, and its chill made her shudder.

This was indeed an unwholesome night, with no

moonlight, and the southerly gale welled with rage. Nightly phantasms took their forms in salty ear-piercing gusts, and ghosts lurked shrieking upon every wave.

"She's holding steady, Captain! Shall I take command?"

Chief Officer Mason was young yet competent. Being a learned young man, he always sought to please *Exodus'* commander, and merchant Captain Connor Arnav was most impressed with his zeal. "Can you handle her?"

An experienced sailor piloted the helm, and both men carefully surveyed. Their powerful voices reached each other as though the thunder and rain only amplified them.

"Aye, Sir," the young man confirmed, smiling upon fearsome waters. "I believe I am capable."

"Very well, then," replied the merchant captain with hidden pride in his apprentice. "I'll be in my cabin."

Those remaining on deck struggled as they went about their tasks, shouting, running, and lighting lamps, but not Connor Arnav. The merchant captain paced his deck with confidence, triumphant over nature and most seamanlike as others braced, each time the hull slammed against the oceans' surface. This tall ship earned her keep as a reputable cargo vessel transporting not only goods but bodies to the United States.

Her captain made a handsome fortune every month, not misusing *Exodus* as an instrument of the slave trade, but of freedom. The vessel's hull consisted primarily of Irish immigrants, eager to escape the blight and the English.

SUMMER ROSE PECK

Connor Arnav, being an American of strong Scotch descent, carried a natural contempt towards the English government in his blood. Robbing 'King and Country' of potentially strong laborers was just as enticing and, if not more than any monetary reward.

Therefore, he found no issues in accepting three pounds and ten shillings a head for ferrying Irishmen and women across the pond; and like the good ship *'Jeanie Johnston,'* no one ever died aboard his vessel. This was the thirty-third night of the crossing. A meager fortnight until New York.

Arnav pranced down the ladder, mindfully and water rushed down the rungs beneath him. In a well-balanced sidestep and entering a deserted passageway, the resonant sounds of a Gaelic tune and laughter rose to his ears from even further below decks.

He shrugged off the gaiety and practically raced into his quarters, not desiring to see another face for a while. Passing the bulkheads which confined his cabin, quietly he shut the door, relieved to be alone, so that he may finally hear his thoughts for the day.

Arnav removed his boat cloak, allowing it to drop from his hands, and fingered certain articles on his desk before collapsing onto his charts in despair. His body managed to find a chair as he allowed himself to fall, and he rested his face on crossed arms.

Sorrow consumed his innermost soul over loss and not the loss over one whom he loved but rather the loss over one whom he loathed. The inability to forgive, he knew was the cause of his woes. "But how?" was always the inescapable question to a seemingly, simplistic resolution.

However, regret soon triumphed, realizing that he neglected to fetch rum before growing comfortable where he was. No matter how loud his mind begged, whined, and cried out for liquor, nothing could uplift him. His heart thumped in agony, no different than the surrounding seas pounding against the keel, and his body felt as weak and heavy as *Exodus'* timbers. This was the way that a man much elder than he should feel, that he knew.

Humming the echoed melodies of '*Drowsy Maggie'* and '*Here's a Health'* managed to lull him into a gentle sleep at times, but he kept waking in disappointment to the unrelenting desire for the bottle. Arnav despised liquor, but it was the only means he had of rest anymore.

Now he raised his dark bearded face from the palms of rough and calloused hands. That mahogany cabinet leered at him in such a way that prevented any means of slumber. Whenever these formidable assailants of grim thoughts came, he countered them with his finest armaments: prayer, the water, animals, and liquor.

Already at sea, no animals about, and having already wished the Savior goodnight, Arnav waved a figurative, white flag and unsteadily, lifted himself from the chair with a sigh, surrendering to the relentless desire.

How the merchant captain managed to keep upright as

he marched to the liquor cabinet was a mystery to him. He could not see the path ahead, although his eyes were widely open. The ship's rolling seemed to assist him along as the motions thrust one leg forward at a time towards his berth.

> Ding, Ding
> Ding, Ding
> Ding, Ding
> Ding. Ding

"Tis midnight now," our merchant captain knew, for the ship's bell, eight times, rang out to signal the mid-watch. "Ah, forget grog," he grumbled, peering into the cabinet's shelves. "Brandy is healthier. Blast…"

In searching for a dram to no avail, he muttered some curses beneath his breath. "The whiskey's out. Whiskey is the only spirit suitable for an icy, miserable night, such as this- Thundering hell! What is that ungodly racket?"

Initially, Arnav assumed a provocation between two Irish gentlemen was the cause for an uproar he heard. A sudden clamor of voices all at once grew still, and the music ceased. "Whatever that was, I have a feeling that it is about to become my problem..."

The merchant captain set out to investigate the commotion and flung open the door to be greeted by Officer Mason, who held a lantern high to his face.

"Had I ever had a son, he'd be identical to Mason,"

theorized the merchant captain and with woe at being a bachelor. Arnav was quite fond of his chief officer and felt fatherly towards him. Mason's gentle mix of light and swarthy features reminded him very much of the sailor he once was many years ago.

The young man mumbled, "Captain," three times in his flawless Maine-man accent before being urged to get to the point with a stark stare.

"Captain, my apologies for disturbing you," said he and nervous. "Tis not my fault, Captain, I swear it. I – I…" Arnav held up a hand to quiet him.

"What is the trouble, Officer Mason? What was that ruckus I just heard?"

"Captain, we - I didn't mean to frighten her, but she-"

"Who?"

"A young lady, Sir," he replied, "a stowaway. Below, some of the ladies began to question her out of suspicion. Seaman Porter called me down to ask how the situation should be dealt with, and well-"

"Breathe, Mister Mason."

"I am sorry, Sir. I ran all the way here," the young man panted and, without realizing it at times, emulating his commander's infectious Scottish diction.

"Well, Sir, when I came down, she got frightened and ran. I don't know where she intends to go," he chuckled a moment and straightened his posture, having finally caught his breath. "I am very concerned for her safety… I did not mean to frighten her, Captain, honest I didn't. Speaking freely, I would be glad to pay her way. I think she is a runaway. She seemed quite desperate and -"

"Where is she now?"

Our merchant captain grew worried, his voice firmer, and snatched the lamp hanging on the nearest bulkhead.

"Well, that is just it, Sir, I do not know. We have men searching for her all over the ship, but she - she's really spooked, Captain."

Arnav threw an arm across the man's chest, pushed him aside, and rushed past.

"Captain," the officer spoke after him. "I believe she actually thinks we are going to throw her overboard or put her to work or something. The poor thing is terrified of us." Together, Arnav and his first officer gazed down separate passageways.

"Have the men search all the compartments, Officer Mason. Did you not happen to catch said girl's name?"

"No, Sir, but I do know that she is quite a beauty," he laughed, stroking his muttonchops but soon regretted his untimely humor. "Forgive me, Sir, merely a jest."

"Go below," Arnav commanded unamused. "And make certain the passengers are not squabbling over this. The last thing I need is for them to start lodging complaints."

"Aye, Sir!" the chief officer answered, racing down a hatch and the merchant captain called after him.

"Wait, Mason?"

"Yes Sir?"

"Who is at the helm?"

"The Second Officer, Sir. Officer Pettigrew."

"I change me mind," he spoke on the verge of a migraine. "Go back on deck and relieve Pettigrew. Have him go below to deal with the bloody passengers. Your skills are better equipped than his in foul weather."

The Chief Officer nodded and smiled, having felt honored at such a compliment from his captain.

"Aye, Sir!" Emerging from the hatch, Mason bolted through the port gangway.

In the absence of their voices, Arnav heard the ship creek all over. The starboard gangway before him was wet and unlit. He had a sensation no different than that of a child striding down a dark hallway at night with nothing but a flickering candle to light the path.

One may hear many a groan and wail off a vessels' timbers that do not seem to be made by the living, be it a living being or a living gale. *Exodus'* moaning warned of malevolent things both imminent and portentous.

Our merchant captain marched on regardless, lantern in hand, adjusting the placement of his seal-skin boots to the ship's never-ceasing roll. Some often believe that the wind can only howl, but at sea, it whistles, and it did so now with anger in its resonance overwhelming all who hear it.

This man lived much of his life at sea. He served in the United States Navy for a spell, went on to become a whaler, and yet even now, as a member of the merchant service, these sounds still manage to fright him.

Silently, he stomped through the thin layer of water splashing from side to side on the shipboards. Sailors could be heard all over, storming through the lower decks, but Arnav believed the girl was somewhere near the main deck based on his knowledge of the ship's build.

Ahead was the ladder, and some seawater continued to surge through its hatch.

"I left the cloak in my cabin," he remembered with rue and grew more frustrated. "Hopefully, the girl isn't on deck- damn it!"

Beneath his feet, an animal lay hidden, who wailed in panic when the merchant captain stumbled over him. Below, Black Jackson crossed his path, hissing. The creature glowered at him and caterwauled a little more before scurrying off.

"Devilish cur!" the merchant captain roared. "I thought I left you in Ireland! Vicious little wretch…"

Exodus housed many cats, and Arnav loved them as he loved all animals. All animals save for this one.

Seaman Dawson appropriately named the cat 'Black Jackson' after the fearsome defender of New Orleans. As the name implied, the animal was ebony furred and, in addition, possessed green, glaring eyes, which were the only means of seeing him in the dark. Black Jackson's nature was violent, and affection he held towards none.

THE MERCHANT & MARINA

"I guess the little fiend has more important things to do than claw flesh from my bones tonight. I'd throw him overboard if it wasn't such bad luck...."

Humbled by the enraged six-pound animal, Arnav breathed in deeply and turned aft into the gangway. On his way down the corridor to fetch the cloak, he perceived gentle footsteps in the water several yards aft.

"Tis the girl, I'll wager," mumbled he to himself.

The merchant captain hung the lantern on a hook and walked back to peek around the corner. Slowly he strode, allowing his eyes some time to see through the night's veil. All he observed was the ladder when he peered around the corner but gazed beyond it to see movement. A figure arose from behind a grouping of barrels.

Why Arnav didn't approach her immediately, he knew not. Speculating on her background arrested him a while, for he had seen so many stowaways now of late that it was starting to become a game.

"What misfortune has brought this one to me, I wonder? Abuse, poverty, the law, hunger pangs?"

He faulted none for fleeing an unpleasant situation under just circumstances, but, at times, Captain Connor Arnav shook his head at the poor fools wanting to buy up land, even if it was in the States, and often pitied stowaways for their desperation. Seeking out more land to escape oppression, Arnav believed foolish as a seafaring man.

"Nature provided mankind with such a vast ocean not to

go unexplored and yet," his mind rambled with rhetoric.

"Nature, likewise, provided mankind an entire continent, free and separated from both sides of the world by oceans, to allow an escape from despotism as well."

For our merchant captain, all these thoughts passed in mere moments, for they were topics he thought on often.

"But tyranny shall one day come onto the United States just the same as any other land. For tyranny can even spread unto water through warships. At least on the water, there are better methods of evasion…"

She seemed accustomed to the lack of light, but he could only discern her shape, seemingly wondering what direction in which to go. Taking a deep breath, he rounded the corner to confront her.

"Miss?"

When Arnav faced her, she quickly raised a lantern, newly lit high to the face, startled. Her visage glowed in the light of the flame, but the rest of her looks were dimmed.

It was a European-looking face, pale and perhaps no more than twenty years old, but the eyes were of the isles. Her eyes, unblinking, were indistinguishable between blue and green. She was dressed entirely in black and wore no scarf or bonnet to secure her nut-brown locks.

There was an inner dismay and ominous look about her countenance that gave Arnav a deep feeling of trepidation. Little did he know that this face would soon be forged in his memories alongside many other phantoms.

"Miss?"

Being cornered, she took a step back and said nothing.

"Miss, it is alright. No one is going to harm you."

The merchant captain sought to approach her, calmly as one would a wounded deer, fearful that she would do something rash like charge up the ladder.

"Miss, please come with me," he entreated once more, but his words had no effect.

It is said that one can predict a person's actions within a second depending on which direction their eyes will go, and the stowaway's eyes darted towards the ladder. With that single motion, Arnav knew her course.

"Miss, don't!"

Just as her eyes foretold, the stowaway girl bolted to the ladder, petticoat fluttering beneath her frock, and mounted each step as swiftly as a doe, never missing a step.

"Miss, no! It's dangerous! Come back! … Damn!"

Arnav ran after her and climbed up the ladder onto the main deck in a trot just as skillfully as she.

Once our merchant captain planted a first step topside, he was immediately slammed on the planks. *Exodus* demanded a reckoning with the North Atlantic. Her bow struck the swells madly atop each mountainous wave.

Ahead he saw the girl wrestling in the arms of Officer Pettigrew in full foul weather gear. The second officer subdued her, but she grappled, determined to break loose from his grip.

The second officer held her in his arms, protectively and in a tight lock as they both fell to the planks just as Arnav did at the shock. *Exodus* wailed like a banshee in her war cry against the elements and, now she began to slide, ready to meet the next onslaught.

Again, the captain fell forward, drenched and Officer Pettigrew, at last, lost his grip on the stowaway girl. Managing to regain balance, he shouted to Pettigrew, but the gale grew deafening. Up until this time, the winds had only served to elevate their voices, yet now, they contrived against our weary merchant captain.

The deckhands endeavored to perform well, though they were sorely tired of being wet. Their hands ached from holding on for dear life and hoped their grip would hold out just a little while longer.

"Drop the anchor!" the chief officer ordered, and another command from Arnav quickly followed. "Reef the topsails! Get aloft!"

These seasoned sailors fought vigorously, as never before and incessantly, to regain control of the vessel. They were truly frightened of the ocean's elements and secretly readied themselves for a quick and speedy surrender to her wrath.

"She's holding steady!

"Keep her steady, lads!"

The merchant captain gripped Pettigrew's shoulder and dragged the man so that his ear went close to his mouth.

"Where is she?!"

Pettigrew likewise took Arnav to his shoulder. "I do not know, Sir! I cannot see her anywhere!"

"Go below and see to the passengers! I'll go after the girl!"

"Aye, Captain! Wait, here, Sir!" The second officer pulled off his raincoat and tossed it to Arnav. "Give this to her! And Godspeed, Sir!"

Meanwhile, Officer Mason clutched the helm, watching the entire scene play out. He spotted the girl, relinquishing control of the ship's wheel to Seaman Dawson, and flayed his arms like one possessed to get the captain's attention.

Once Arnav saw him, the chief officer directed him with a point of hand larboard, past the foc'sle, shouting, "she's there! She's there!"

Arnav hardly heard the man but understood his meaning. He hastened along the way, feeling the wood shudder beneath his boots with every stomp.

Ahead a deckhand caught the girl, but she freed herself yet again and threw herself into Arnav's arms for safety, evading two others. Trembling, it was quite clear she had enough of the Atlantic's fury and acknowledged defeat.

The merchant captain swore he heard the words, "please do not send me back…" carried in a gust with arms tightly draped around him in terror.

Both persons were thoroughly drenched, but he threw the coat over her shoulders anyway by gentlemanly nature.

Petrified, she fingered his shirt collar in an apology of sorts, but he remained stolid and dumbfounded by the foolish lengths she took.

He glared at the young woman with an eye that seemed to inquire, 'are you insane?'

Yet she appeared so innocent to him and so full of rue that he knew he would never be able to upbraid her.

"So young... Too young to be making a journey such as this by herself," he thought with distress and sighed breathless in pondering his next course of action. "Far too young... I might just have to pay her way myself."

In one long flash of lightning, the woman's face fixed into his mind like a photograph. A mindful photograph that would not soon tear. Captain Arnav forced his escapee into an 'about face' towards the ladder, but promptly seized her hand yet again.

"BRACE!"
Ding, Ding, Ding...
"BRACE!"
Ding, Ding, Ding...
"BRACE YOURSELVES, LADS!"
Ding, Ding, Ding...
"HOLD FAST TO THE RIGGING!"

Mason clanged the ship's bell wildly in warning to Arnav, and our merchant captain turned his head to see an immense crest forming on the waves.

Eyes widened, the girl hurled the weight of the coat off her shoulders and struggled to free herself from the captain, who seemed entranced by the imminent behemoth. Men on the shrouds remained motionless, shut their eyes, and gripped the ratlines as their lives depended on it.

By impulse, she pulled away from him. She trusted her legs to get her to the ladder, and indeed they were swift, but Arnav knew far better the ways of his deceiving sea. Having to fight, he dragged the girl to the bulwarks in a desperate effort to likewise cling onto a line.

Exodus ascended in seconds, and bursting, through the peak, she propelled her crew into the air. A burst of white water fell like snow upon the decks, only colder and harder. The impact against the waves bruised *Exodus,* and the forceful rush of the water that swept over the planks threw the girl off her feet.

Arnav felt the woman's hand being ripped from his by nature's passions. The men were heavier and more accustomed to the briny barrage, but the woman's delicate figure was swept away from his grasp and went over the rail screaming all the way down.

She plummeted into the unforgiving swells of the North Atlantic, and Arnav looked on in horror at her dire plunge.

"PASSENGER OVERBOARD!"

SUMMER ROSE PECK

Several sailors charged to the stern lanterns in hands and hurled a cask buoy over the ship. The merchant captain followed, staggering.

"HELP!"
"HELP!"

Each desperate cry for help began to fade in the tempestuous winds. As thoroughly as the men scanned the churning white surface, none could see her, even though her frantic cries for assistance were profoundly heard by them all. "SWIM FOR THE BUOY!" the sailors yelled into the black night. "SWIM FOR THE BUOY!"

"Captain, Captain," shouted the helmsman. "Should we come about? Should we come about, Sir?!"

The helmsman received no answer, and the crew exchanged glances of staunch disapproval. "We've veered enough! Steer her portside any further, and she'll list!"

"Are you daft?!" many proceeded to cry in uproar. "We'll founder if we come about! The pumps will fail!"

"Don't you dare turn that wheel, Dawson!" another warned with harrowing sincerity.

"I'm asking the captain!"

"STICK TO OUR COURSE, SEAMAN DAWSON!"

Arnav roared in delay and practically choked on his own words. One young man clapped his ears, unable to listen to her cries any longer, and implored Heaven for her.

Another, a cabin boy tied a sheet around his waist, ready to dive into the fathoms after her, but the crew prevented the brave lad in his efforts, reserved and grim.

"Nay, she is lost, Captain!" Officer Gregg pronounced firmly and declared, "I do not see her anywhere!"

Arnav threw his cap down violently upon the deck and muttered profane words to himself, slumping with a tight grasp on the taffrail. His heart pumped with such intensity that the sound reached his ears, and breaths of air seemed hard to come by. The girl was gone, swallowed by the passage that has claimed so many souls.

His men felt just the same as he, angry and disappointed with themselves, but stayed reserved. Sincerely now, they wished for Arnav's rank so that they might likewise have the liberty to reveal their solace with such dignity as Arnav displayed.

Their captain never lost his composure throughout some gesticulating, and only he could swear so eloquently like one composing a poem. A true and living embodiment of the word 'sailor.'

"Officer Mason!"

Mason approached Arnav, tentative and the captain placed a hand on the younger man's shoulder in exhaustion. "Mason," he muttered miserably. "I shall be in my cabin logging all of this down. I have many papers to write. I do not wish to be disturbed for the remainder of this dreadful night." Last he ordered, "maintain our heading."

SUMMER ROSE PECK

The thunder resonated once more throughout the night, and it was the last *Exodus* heard of it for the remainder of the voyage once Arnav returned to his quarters.

CHAPTER TWO

THE BOATHOUSE

It was upon a drizzly night in the port of St. Augustine, Florida, where the curious haunting of the retired merchant Captain 'Connor Arnav' began. The year was 1845, and the month was May.

The rain fell softly upon his overcoat as he passed Trinity Parish, but a fierce battle raged in the Heavens, and the wind wailed. Lightning tinted the skies white in flashes, and thunder shook the very ground upon which Arnav strode.

A landsman would have been frightened of the seas' pounding against the sands, but the wrath of the ocean was all that Arnav ever lived for, terrifying though it was. Akin to a woman lavishing tears, he once believed that when rains fell with such an anguish, it was a warning to all who inhabit a seaside that only the boldest of seamen may enter the ocean's domain unscathed.

Calm and tearful tempests such as these once soothed his soul but afforded him minimal relief to his misery now. Tonight, was particularly fretful.

Why? He knew not, but the eerie wails which the weatherly gale brought to shore seemed to be an echo of wails from all those who have long since perished on the foam. The waves sweeping the docks were a constant reminder of clashes with Poseidon, who had been his lifelong adversary.

Over the decades, he contented with frightful storms that contrived to flounder his vessels on many a voyage. Numerous battles Arnav had won, others he had lost, but his war with the sea was still raging and still his victory for as long as he was alive and breathing.

His arms remained tightly interlocked over his brass-buttoned coat, with one hand gripped on a bottle of stout, and his Aegean capped head was down. This American sea captain, a son of migrated Scots, ambled handsomely at over six feet and four inches in height.

Although raised upon North Carolinian streets, his sturdy speech remained dominantly with the Scottish in thanks to a Scot Vicker and orphan keeper.

The hairs which graced his head and face were faded chestnut. His immersive eyes were richer than Tahitian black pearls, and his skin was forever tanned the shade of wet sand. Designs inherited to him by a life of grueling labor under the merciless sun and an Indian ancestor.

Well-formed features such as his did not imply by any means that he was a vexed man, but his appealing face was lamentably scarred, like boulders by the sea at the relentless onslaught of squalls beyond their mastery. As salt to iron, it is said by many that hatred is the most damaging emotion, and Arnav had much of it.

On some nights, hatred, regret, and despair were all that seized his mind and soul, and this was one of those unfortunate nights he had to endure.

In defiance of the dreary London-like setting, the weather remained as it always was in the south of Florida, warm. Gazing at the stark skies, additionally, he wondered, while walking home from the tavern, if this would be the unfortunate day that he would finally be struck by lightning. A man of forty-seven years, Arnav feared no man nor storm, but even now, the thought of being struck by lightning had been his sincerest and most irrational fear he cherished ever since a young man.

Aye, this night was particularly fretful. Why? He knew not. Something inside simply felt uneasy, but the warm liquor surging down his throat forced most of his fears to melt away.

Wooden signs about him creaked, bellowing at the powerful gusts. The steeple bells overhead the church moaned in agony, and dogs bayed as though they sensed the presence of the supernatural.

Treading through puddles in the street, he passed many homes and businesses of Cuban refugees until he came upon a hidden trail amidst a grove of palms that forked off the main road. Our grim merchant captain marched steadily through his forest of fronds and for some time until arriving upon a secluded beach on the mouth of Matanzas River, overlooking Anastasia Island.

The foliage was so thick that if a castaway washed ashore and hadn't walked a little way, he'd assume himself forever lost on a deserted island.

Captain Arnav's beach kept hidden from all, secluded a shabby yet sturdy boathouse, canopied by massive palms and marsh. He could thrive no place else. The company of others bothered him unless they were fellow seamen or tavern dwellers, and sleep alluded him in the absence of breakers.

To Arnav, however, this hideous, hastily built driftwood boathouse was a palace and indeed home. Its ghastly appearance contrasted sufficiently with the surrounding tropical features and blended somewhat agreeably in the Caribbean fashion.

It satisfied all his wants and housed not only himself but the '*Seminole.*' The roof of this boathouse covered both his home and the slip for his vessel, having a kind of inner dock, in a manner of speaking.

THE MERCHANT & MARINA

Alas, Arnav was no longer the merchant captain of a fine tri-masted barque and countless crewmen, but rather the commander of a pathetic fishing dinghy and no crewmen other than a mongrel dog. Seldom was it that he ever journeyed too far out on the drink nowadays and exclusively for the purpose of fishing. That was his trade now. A merchant of tarpons and snappers.

This piece of land and sea lashed together was indeed his sanctuary. Visitors were expressly forbidden, and guests were strictly prohibited from entering his paradise, and so, unbeknown was the fearless Connor Arnav to the guest already awaiting him there.

With much effort and plodding through the thick sand, he found his scruffy pet outside, snarling at the door. The barking mongrel attempted to warn his master about an intruder, but Arnav was sorely doubtful.

"What are you doing out here? Go on!" his master bellowed. "Go on! Go use the door I built for you!" Arnav felt acclimated to shouting over the water. His voice commanded the skies like the thunder itself, and ill winds turned their tails at its resonance.

Arnav's dog whined at the scolding and shook his tail in apology but kept grimacing. His focus remained steadfast with the door, and nothing would sway him from his duty. There was an unwelcome creature in his master's home, and that was all the mongrel understood.

"Oh, stop your grousing, Hector," he growled, impatient.

The sea captain felt unconvinced of danger, for 'Hector' had the tendency to bark at all noises.

"My dog, the one who cries wolf," presumed he and ushered the dog away from the door. "Perhaps there be a snake or some other critter within. Oh well, tis no matter. He'll grouse and bay until he actually meets such a creature and scurry away."

Loath to lay his hand upon the door, Arnav grew tense and carefully shoved the door open as its hinges were rusty, and he had procrastinated many days in cleaning them. Of course, it would not open with one push, and so he burst through, impatient to get out of the rain. Meanwhile, the dog cried, insistent that his master should not enter the dwelling, and begged him to reconsider.

Light the man required, but light there was none. Reaching for a lamp that hung beside the door, a sudden splash made him jump. Hector barked, growled, and whined, all at once but aptly made a retreat out the door, abandoning his master. The intuitive animal sensed some troubling presence in the waters of the boathouse.

"Must be a shark or fish trapped underneath the deck," was the sea captain's first assumption, straining his eyes. "And a massive one at that."

Striking a match from his desk, he carefully peered into the restless waters that encompassed the Seminole.

Ding, Ding

THE MERCHANT & MARINA

Ding, Ding
Ding, Ding
Ding, Ding.

No man was more acclimated to a ship's bell than Arnav. He had heard it so many times at sea during his life's history that he didn't even think to question the origin of which there was none.

The lightning grew more thunderous, yet he perceived a voice. A human-sounding voice which made his very soul writhe with terror and his blood run cold as the clock on the bulkhead struck twelve.

"Eight bells, Captain Arnav," spoke a stranger in a feminine tenor.

Startled, he found lighting the lamp to be a grueling task. His hands were trembling so, and he refused to ease the grasp on the bottle's neck in his other hand. But fumbling, he eventually managed to light the lantern and illuminated the boathouse.

At the sight of what he saw, his limbs went numb, his knees shook, and he dropped the bottle, where it promptly fell to the deck with a sharp clash. The glass shattered, scattering in a thousand pieces.

Never had Arnav committed such as sin as releasing his liquor, and at that moment, he felt stone-cold sober, leaning against the bulkhead in shock.

"My God… It's her…"

CHAPTER THREE

THE

SURVIVOR

The ocean was such that one could see its brutal surface extend for miles. In the month of June 1813, the War of 1812 was raging on the Atlantic, strong as ever and without remorse. This man's career at sea began as prisoner of war.

Droplets of salt water might just as well have been grains of sand on a desert. This was one of those sweltering days at sea where you never saw the sun but felt its wrath even from its hiding place beyond the clouds. The air smelt heavily of gun powder and American and British blood streaked the deck.

THE MERCHANT & MARINA

HMS Magister, N. coast off North Carolina
Compliment:305 souls
Armament: 38 guns
Orders: Intercept and aid HMS Junon off coast of Hampton, Virginia, to receive further orders. Supply her with fresh hands and provisions. Expect to be welcomed by American gunboats.

The Union Jack refused to flutter and hung solemn amongst the masts that still stood on the 'heavy' frigate, *HMS Magister*. This vessel had taken substantial damage from an intense battle with the now vanquished, *USS Gallant*. The American frigate undermanned with her thirty-two guns was no match for the even heavier and superior British man o' war.

Gallant's crew had been split days before to sail a captured British schooner to Ontario in perhaps the worst timing fathomable. On the main deck and facing the stern, six surviving American sailors were kept on their knees, shackled, and burning on deck at the point of their captors' 'Brown Bess' - The name English sailors and Royal Marines affectionately refer to as their muskets.

"She swooped in on us like a vulture," the first mate whispered, fidgeting with the hot irons round his wrists. "Anyhow, I've heard that he is an eloquent man, Captain."

Boone was the first of the prisoners that dared to speak after being captured. No words were shared amongst their conquerors, nor further commands given, and not even a gull screeched. Much of the crew were busy in making repairs below decks. Their labors and creaking remained the dominant sounds throughout the hull, as the ship ominously rolled back and forth on gentle waves.

"If that be so then we are indeed doomed men, Master Boone," replied his undefeated commander. "If there is anything I have learned about the damned English, and mankind in general, is that the more eloquent they are, the more vicious in nature."

Enveloped by heat, several prisoners of war collapsed from heat exhaustion, on the verge of death. Yet their cruel captors kept on watching them with emotionless glances.

The newly imprisoned, Captain George Washington Lange was not about to lose heart, however. To a native Virginian, 'beaten' was a blasphemous word against a proud southern heritage. He was a romantic of sorts, swathed by tales of honor and loyalty to creeds. He prided himself on being a man of the sea, a musician, and a philosopher who knew of no such word as 'defeat.'

His posture was unbreakable despite a desperate thirst for shade and his face was rigid as stone, even while the grief over the loss of his beloved frigate and shipmates to the enemy was utterly, unbearable. He appeared proud even while being forced to his knees in surrender.

The boy seaman shackled to the captain's left, Connor Arnav, knew that John Paul Jones himself could not have been braver than Captain Lange. No man else came closer to being his father, other than Lange. Under no obligation to, this man had taught him how to steer, sail, and navigate. Skills that Arnav would apply throughout the course of his life and felt forever indebted to him for them.

Therefore, he would never come to forget the terrorizing last moments he was to share with the man who had been his mentor or the remaining shipmates whom he considered to be no less than his brothers, even if they never thought so themselves.

"Captain, where will they take us?"

"The brig," Lange answered musingly, and the cabin boy was silent, thereafter, aside from a few hoarse coughs.

"I do not know, Son," he clarified, blowing dark hairs, and sweat away from his eyes.

"To Deadman's Island, more than likely," an able seaman at the far end of the line grimly spoke. Seaman Becker was busy in attending to a heat-stricken shipmate and found it difficult to revive him. "Or Dartmoor Prison."

"You trying to frighten him, for God's sake, Becker?"

"Nay, Mr. Droves, but I think it be only fair that he knows the truth."

Connor took short stabbing breaths out of fear until the captain urged composure. "Do not worry, Mister Arnav," he whispered steadily and looked the young man directly in the eyes. "The reputation of Melville's Island is exaggerated. You are still young. Scottish blood runs through your veins, and Mr. Becker is of English parentage. They might just be easier on the two of you."

"Or worse!"

Regardless of Becker's rebuke, this confident answer from the captain reassured the young man for the time being. Yet, Captain Lange possessed the ability to keep calm while overcome with great stress.

Privately, he found the conduct of this crew highly unusual, even for the British. The faces of these men alone suggested they were scoundrels and sorely undisciplined ones at that.

Their behavior appeared barbaric in the way they circled the deck, and the prisoners, awaiting a decision to be reached by their commanders.

"If we were to be placed in the brig, then we would have been thrown in there immediately after being taken aboard," Lange concluded mindfully.

"These men are vengeful and for what purpose I know not, other than the general. We are Americans. Perhaps, we are not bound for Deadman's Island. We may be headed towards a far more merciful fate..." And at this time, George Lange dearly wished to have the portrait of his wife now so that he may grip it in preparation for Judgment, but alas, it went down with his ship.

Donned in a uniform that Satan would envy, Captain Fox emerged from his cabin wearisome, with warrant officers following close behind; their deliberations done.

"Have the carpenter brought to me," was the captain's first bid to a midshipman. "I want a damage report."

While similarly patterned to the previous state of the prisoners' naval blue uniforms, the officers of the Royal Navy wore theirs in a contemptible and gaudier fashion.

Never was there a name more suited to a man than Captain Edward Fox. For like the hide of a fox, his hair was blood red, with a pair of eyes that were the shade of rust. His lips were long and thin, no different than that same animal's sly grin, and his words, they were cold. Piercingly cold, as though he could not feel the scolding from the sun which the clouds now birthed.

"Our Empire," he addressed Lange with a sharp, Bristolian tongue, "has captured the *USS Chesapeake* under the command of a Captain James Lawrence. You know the man?"

"I cannot say that I do personally," returned Lange coolly though accompanied by the sun's intense glare. "I know of him. Many know of him."

"Oh, what a shame. Anyhow, I thought you would appreciate to know that he died and not pleasantly either." A select few of *Magister's* crew grinned like jubilant wolves, proud of their leader's cruelty.

"We have also secured the *Chesapeake* in thanks to our beloved *Shannon*," he added braggingly.

"My men are in need of medical assistance," Lange stated, and quite carefully. "Have you a ship's surgeon?"

"I had one. He was killed by your vessel's guns in the barrage."

"May we speak in your cabin?"

"Nay, Captain Lange. You will all stay where you are."

"Then at least throw us in the brig!" Boone shouted in agony. "You cannot torture us like this!"

Swiftly, the man was struck down with the bud end of a musket, and Lange gazed upon his writhing crew member feeling helpless.

"Apparently, I can," Fox replied over the sailor's groaning. Aside from deploying reason, Lange saw no other way of cheating fate. "Captain Fox, according to the articles of war and the law of the Admiralty -"

"I do not see the Admiralty here, do you, Captain?"

Lange eyed Fox, speechless, but his mind was far from silent. "When many wicked men combine, merciless acts weigh nothing upon their conscience because they bear the weight of their crimes together," he remembered.

"In the end, there is no rationalizing with men who are uncivil and pure evil. Nor is there any use in hating them either. Thank God I cannot understand this man. For to do that, I would have to be no different than him."

"Your reserve is commendable, Captain Lange," Fox stated in a vile tone. "Do you not wish to make an outcry?" Lange saw the devilish disappointment in Fox's face and kept quiet. Becker, though a good sailor, was a slow man and could not yet see the reality of their situation. "What –

what do you mean to do with us, then?"

"Isn't it obvious, Becker?" The imprisoned quartermaster spoke up, who had all this time remained silent and in painful contemplation. Pure hopelessness was writ deep into his frown.

The survivors began to mumble amongst themselves and plead for mercy. "Mercy, Captain!"

"Please, mercy!"

"Mercy, Captain Fox!"

"Please!"

Several wept hysterically and could not gather any words, but Becker's epitaph was a renunciation of his oath and allegiance to the states in a degrading attempt at self-preservation. "God save the King!" he yelled and groveled. "Spare me, my native countrymen!"

"COWARD!" the others cried with murderous rage.

"BLATANT COWARDICE!"

"PITIFUL!"

"DAMN YOU, BECKER!"

"TRAITOR!"

"Captain," Lange's southern draw wavered and without a thought to Becker's disavowal. "I beg of you at least spare the boy. He's only fifteen!"

Fox shifted his back to the men, mounting the quarter-deck and from this height, he pronounced a death sentence for his prisoners. "Let it be written in the log. There were no survivors of the *Gallant*!"

Some were in the middle of prayer, others genuflected, but most of the prisoners screamed in vain when British bayonets skewered their bodies.

With tears swelling in his eyes, Lange simply whispered his wife's name, "Miranda..." before he met his end, falling face-first into the scolding planks.

It was not long before five American sailors lay on the deck dead to brutal British hands. Only the cabin boy had been spared, but he wailed out of immense terror and writhed on deck.

Feverishly the carpenter raced up the quarterdeck to speak with his commander and shuffled to. "Minor hull damage, Captain. We're patching her up right now."

"Can she sail? Our orders are to meet with the *Junon*. I do not wish to miss her."

"Aye, Sir. We believe so, Sir," was the carpenter's answer. "Much of the damage is superficial. *Gallant's* aim and timing was considerably off..."

"Excellent..." he whispered as a gust began to brew. "Master Holland!"

"Aye, Sir?"

"Add this in the ship's books on Gallant's sinking. Only ONE survivor was pulled from the water. A boy seaman, half-drowned and nearly dead. Get his name later."

"Aye, Sir."

With hesitation in his face but an undeniable urge to relish in his triumph over the Americans, Fox marched down the steps to face the boy. Arnav covered his eyes and did not wish to meet his gaze. Peeking through his fingers, Arnav saw Fox's legs first, which were short and slender. This depraved monster reminded him very much of the painting he once saw of Napoleon.

"Get up, Boy," he commanded quietly.

Arnav gripped the planks, emotionally paralyzed. Never in his wildest dreams could he contemplate such villainy. Ere he braved the sea cruelty was the very thing he sought refuge from in great earnest.

"Now, I say!"

Still, the boy remained face down on deck and bit his lip, not about to show any further displays of weakness. Impatient and enraged, Fox dragged Arnav up by his hair and hurled him unto his feet, unmoved by his panicked whimpers. The captain held him firmly by the neck as one would a newborn whelp and forced the boy to look him directly in his yellowish, narrow-set eyes.

He spat while speaking with his swift, canid-like tongue. "Do you hate me? Do you, wretch?! Good…" Fox nodded as the boy struggled. "You shall need that. Look at them," he ordered, but Arnav wouldn't allow himself to shift.

"Look at them," the captain howled. "Look at them!"

Arnav refused to look at his bloodied crewmates whose souls were now at rest; Boone, Becker, Droves, Smith, and even Lange, but Fox spun him around and forced him to, throwing an arm across the boy's chest.

"Look at them! Do you want to end up like them? Remember it! The next American vessel we meet, you will go to her and tell them *Magister* will show no quarter! You will tell them exactly what happened here! Master Mann! Get some men to clean this up!" he commanded with flaying arms. "All hands to stations! Get us underway! Bring her up on the wind, Nor by Norwest!"

Seaman, marines, midshipmen, and officers alike scattered to make sail and spontaneously, as though nothing dire had happened when the boatswain piped up. They cast his lifeless crewmates overboard, and without ceremony, one splash following soon after another.

Arnav silently prayed in murmurs. He thought per chance, that he had seen one or two English sailors disturbed by this sight, regret in their eyes, mumbling "Heavenly Father…" but was never entirely sure.

Overwrought with a lust for vengeance, young Arnav continued to struggle. Summoning some courage, he tried to resist and escape this devil's grip to no avail.

"Bastard!" he cried. The captain slapped the boy across the face with a free hand and threw him into the arms of the ship's disheveled boatswain. "HERE! Give him some work to do with the other boys!"

The man whispered, "come on, Lad," almost with a node of sympathy, before marching him below decks.

"He's a prisoner of war, Captain," the first lieutenant argued in Fox's ear. "Same as any other. I do not like this plan. It is incredibly risky. You seriously do not mean to give him back to the Americans as a warning?"

"I might if given the opportunity."

"If he tells the Americans what we have done, and they believe him, it could lead to an inquiry."

"You did not seem too concerned about that when we were deciding on it, Lieutenant Yates. Besides, that is precisely what I want him to do. It will instill just the right amount of fear and further *Magister's* reputation amongst the most superstitious of our enemies."

"We should have wrung the boy's neck as far as I am concerned or let him swing from the yardarm. Did you not hear him speak? He is Scotch by birth, therefore a traitor."

"Trust me, Yates. No one will believe him. No one of any importance, that is."

"What if he finds a way to testify against us?"

"It will be my word against his, then!"

The sails were raised, the wheel commanded, and thus the officers felt the ship suddenly thrust forward beneath them as wind filled the canvas. The crew resumed swabbing blood off the decks and repairing the damage around them. Work on a ship was never done, and the stress in their voices resounded loud and crude.

"Let us drink to our victory, Yates," Fox declared, guiding his first mate over to the rail, subtly, with a hand upon his shoulder. "Tonight, we shall assemble all the senior officers in my cabin."

They glanced about to ensure none were listening in on their conversation, even if it was an unnecessary precaution. Many of these men were just as callous themselves and most likely could not care if they did not already know of the officers' blatant schemes.

"If we send him back, not everyone will believe him. Trust me on that, Yates. Oh, amateur seamen and vengeful officers may believe him at first, out of their hatred for us, but my naval career is pristine. What intelligent man of a high-ranking position would believe such a horrid thing about me after I was merciful enough to send a young survivor back to his people rather than sending him to a place like Halifax? Or Dartmoor?"

"What if some do?" the mate maliciously countered.

"I have influential friends, and in both countries," Fox whispered, grinning. "It is remarkable how feeble-minded Americans are. We shall stick to our course, so to speak. If this gale turns into a tempest, we shall ride it out as any other storm, with smiles and flattery."

CHAPTER FOUR

THE MERMAID

There she was. An apparition risen from the depths. "This must be the sea's answer to a ghost," Arnav affirmed in great terror. A creature with the head and midriff of a beautiful woman but the bottom half of a fish. A haunting image of the same nameless stowaway maid who drowned on one of his crossings.

He lowered the lantern to gaze into her face, and surely enough, it was inexplicably familiar. The mysterious wraith hoisted herself unto the deck, water streaming from her tanned skin and sun-kissed brunette hair, but Arnav could only observe her tail, hanging half in and half out of the water in fearful envy.

"Dost, thou know who I am, Connor Arnav?"

"No-no," he lied. "No! Get out! Leave me!"

"I am she, whom five years ago this very night thou didst allow to die at sea."

"Get out!" he cried, falling back again and grief in his face whispered, "what manner of treachery is this?"

Our merchant captain believed this encounter was to be one of that, like the old parable of the 'blind and deaf boatman' who came for you at any time he pleased. That this siren, undoubtedly was about to and at any moment, snatch him off the deck of his boathouse.

That he was to be dragged beneath the darkest depths of the sea, his flesh consumed by all manner of marine creatures, and his soul ferried straight on to hell.

"But you are dead," he poorly rationalized. "I've drunk heavily and from the wrong bottle tonight…"

"I am not a figment of thy mind's eye."

Hers was a deceiving voice, sounding American in deliverance, when indeed it was an English voice of the south-east midlands, which resonated so softly. Arnav recognized all accents of the isles.

"That's-that's not possible. I- I saw you die! What are you? Some demon or some devil haunting me now?!"

"Marina was my name," she said and motioned with a wave of her hand. "Set down thy lantern and be not affrighted. Come hither and sit by me."

THE MERCHANT & MARINA

"Why?!"

A smirk formed over the creature's lovely face, which frightened him. "Thou art curious, Captain. Do not deny it." And once more, she gently motioned with her palm. "Surely, thou are not frightened of a spirit?"

Arnav paced angrily as his pride was wounded. Without employing, any words, Marina had asked him for his trust and, without answering, the captain contemplated the unspoken request.

Finally, and never removing his eyes from hers, Arnav decided to approach Marina but dragged the chair from his desk while doing so to implement as a possible weapon. Shifting the chair, slowly he sat down, near the edge of the slip, and sank down.

Now he saw Marina more clearly. Myriad scales graced certain areas of her body and were only visible on her skin in the flickering from the lamplight. Two white scalloped seashells were fixed across her chest for modesty by means of strap from a tattered fishing net.

The angles in the face were rounded sharply and to the captain appeared, dare he thought, sharkish. Her tail was iridescent, silver, and speckled, no different than that of a tarpon. The fluke he didn't see, for foam eddied about it.

The eyes that he had first seen on *Exodus* were the same, indistinguishable between blue and green like the shade of Floridian waves. Droplets of water continued to fall from her waist-long hair and skin, but she made no effort to help them along.

"Yes, Marina," he answered her calmly and gulped. "I remember you now. I often wondered what your name was."

"Drown me, consume me, or drag me down?" Whether it was one or all these acts that were to be committed, Arnav felt dreadfully unprepared. "Christ, protect me," murmured he and with grave earnest.

"Their reputations were far too formidable. Were they not, Captain?"

The man lifted his head in bewilderment, "what?"

"The night I went over *Exodus'* rails, thee despaired over the loss of a man named Yates. A leftenant at the time ye knew him; Commodore Robert Yates of the Royal Navy as the knave came to be known."

"How in bloody hell did you know that?"

"Thy name was bandied about and made a mockery in seeking vengeance, and he managed to cheat it by aging. The last living officer of the *HMS Magister*."

"I meant it last time, and I mean it now," he commanded, rising from the chair. "Get out!"

"For more than three decades ye sought to bring him before justice," she repeated without backing down. "To bring *Magister's* crew before inquiries. They slaughtered thy crewmates and left only thee alive to tell the tale… And yet so few believed thee."

Arnav stumbled to a shelf mum and pulled out another

bottle for emergencies. Whatever this was, it seemed a dire emergency to him. He took a repulsed whiff of the stuff, possibly port, and drank it anyway. "So, thou believest that drowning the flesh with spirits will somehow succeed in drowning the memories within thy soul?"

"No," was his reply and managing not to slur. "But if I drink enough your face is either bound to leave me or I shall pass out and escape from this awful delusion."

Deftly ashamed of himself for cowardice and lack of prowess, the dog returned and through his door to snarl at Marina once more. The mermaid met the animal's gaze and snarled back at him with a snake-like hiss.

Terrified, Hector scurried out just the way he had come, and the merchant captain roared with laughter. "He'll probably go hide in his little hollow for a while. Can you imagine that? I rescued that mongrel to guard me shack!"

Marina observed our bellowing merchant carefully now, arms crossed as he offered her a swig. She declined with a raised palm, respectfully and noticed that Arnav was beginning to enjoy her company.

"Forgive me," begged Arnav while swaying. "I didn't know that mermaids don't drink…"

Thunder clapped when he took the bottle to his lips as though it were a warning to put it down, and so he did, fearfully. "Anyways, you are right. I do not know how you are right, but you are. Few men believed me," he muttered, sinking back into the chair sad.

"Several American politicians and even an admiral apparently had correspondence with *Magister's* wicked commander and knew him long before the war."

"Captain Edward Fox," the mermaid added, and the merchant grew irratible.

"How do you know all of this?! You were not even born when I was fifteen, my dear. Will you not tell me what you are or if you're even real or not? I demand an answer ere I speak further."

"For men of the sea and those lost to it, the ocean hath reserved its own heaven and hell."

"Is that all you are going to tell me? And by men of the sea, you mean-"

"Aye, men such as thyself who believe saltwater pulses through thy veins thicker than blood... Continue with the rest, Captain."

"I spent one hellish week on that murderess they called *Magister*," Arnav recalled and quite reluctant.

"I thought for sure I would soon be on my way to Halifax... She made her way north to the southernmost point of Virginia. On some night in June, American flotillas, militia style, boarded *Magister* and caught her crew by surprise. Unprepared and inexperienced, much of *Magister's* crew were killed in the ambush. There were no casualties on the American's side. That is how fleetly they came and left, and I escaped with them," the man recited, taking another gulp and checked to see if Marina was still offering him a sympathetic ear of which she was.

"Stricken and weak, Fox guided *Magister* into a fog bank. She scampered off like a wounded animal. I later learned after the war that Fox evaded many American vessels and reached Nova Scotia, where *Magister* was repaired. On course there, she received even more casualties by an attack from an American sloop. The much smaller craft boldly took advantage of her wearied state off the coast of Georgetown…"

"Perhaps it was my fault that they didn't believe me when rescued after reciting the horrors that ensued."

Arnav sighed and held the bottle, cradling it with both hands in painful recollection.

"They assumed me delusional from too much sun and saltwater. No trials came up. Not during the war, not after. Some even had the gall to accuse me of slandering Fox as if I would ever concoct such a horrid thing. For those who did believe, it gave them stronger convictions to fight the English, and as for the rest, they were only officers who wanted to believe my story while trying to put an end to a war. They seemed afraid of believing me at times. Afraid to counter the man's reputation. Evidently, he was highly influential at home and abroad."

Shoved in the drawers of his desk, Arnav yanked out a sheet of paper, eager to finally share his deepest woes with someone. "This was Senator Raleigh's public statement to one of my letters in 1816…"

SUMMER ROSE PECK

16th of November 1816,

Now that our second war for independence with Britain has ended and we are victorious, I believe it is only proper to defend the reputation of a man whose name has briefly come into question.

Captain Edward Fox is a man of high standing and much honor in Britain. Though an Englishman, I have personally known his family for many years. It is my deepest conviction that he would never perform such heinous acts as Seaman Connor Arnav describes.

The sinking of the USS Gallant was recounted by Magister's remaining crew to the British Admiralty. All fifty-six surviving men gave an account that the vessel had gone down by the stern in minutes. According to those accounts given, there were no survivors other than the Boy Seaman, Connor Arnav, who seemed delirious when they dragged him out of the water from shock.

Captain George Washington Lange was an honorable man and loyal, devoted to his rank with such a passion that no other officer living could possibly match. It is in my fervid opinion that he and his officers likely chose to go down with their beloved Gallant.

This even the man's venerable widow, Miranda Lange, believes to be true whom I have recently spoken with. I shall personally see to it that the crew of the Gallant are posthumously awarded for their courage and their valor.

THE MERCHANT & MARINA

So, help me, God.

Signed, Senator James H. Raleigh

"For over three decades, thee sought justice. To avenge thy fallen commander and crew and swore retribution against Fox and the rest, but the few remaining after the war kept on dropping."

"Aye, and I finally had Yates. My accusations were finally given some standing in the British Admiralty, and the blaggard had to go and die on me."

Arnav took yet another swig to ease his anguish. "Fox, Yates, and the others all died rich men with high-ranking naval careers, so I've heard. I guess fortune favored them. Whoever it was that said time heals all wounds is a Goddamned liar."

"Villains are heavily rewarded for selling their souls like a condemned man treated to one last meal."

Marina fiddled with a silver scale which fell on the deck boards, unfinished in her resolve. "Whoever it was that said liquor does the same would also have been lying, Captain."

Arnav grumbled a bit to himself in staunch disagreement with the mermaid. Nevertheless, he placed the bottle aside for her sake.

"And yet I pity such men," she stated once more and gazed beyond his woeful eyes. "The insatiable ones. I doubt men like Fox ever knew of such attributes like true love or kindness or compassion. I bet in the whole of his entire life, all he ever felt was thirst. A thirst for power and control that he could never quench."

Our merchant captain observed this mysterious being for a moment and felt moved by her inner wisdom. "Why have you come to me, Marina?"

"Captain Arnav," she replied unwavering and resolute in her tone. "Thou art obsessed with the memory of vile men who have long since passed and met their judgement. That is why I am here. This hatred of thine will most surely destroy thee."

"So, I see, but you did not answer my question. Be there anything else, spirit?"

"Aye, only one thing. Were thee not once a whaler?"

"Aye," Arnav answered almost merrily. "They were the only good years of me life, but that was a very long time ago and an entire world away."

Marina sat there with a sudden 'thou shalt see me at Philippi' look expressed upon a sweetly curved brow.

"I shall leave thee with those thoughts fresh in thy mind then... And I will come to thee again, Connor Arnav at eight bells and again after that until thou art ready for what I have to say. Fare thee well."

"What do you mean by that- wait come back!"

The mermaid dove into the waters beneath the *Seminole,* from whence she came, leaving Arnav astounded. Only now did he ponder the source of the chiming ships' bell.

CHAPTER FIVE

THE WHALERMAN

More often than not, Arnav dreamt of his life past the Cape of Horn but never like this. He was a whaler just as he was in another time. He felt the cold sting of the Arctic air, the pungent odors of a whale's carcass, and once again knew the joy of returning to the crystal blue gentle currents rushing before him on the quartzlike sands of the Pacific.

Again, he remembered how softly the palms swayed against the horizon, how bronzed his hide was and how beautiful Polynesian women were. All the scents, sights, and sounds returned in dreamful reminisces…

SUMMER ROSE PECK

In the summer of 1825, Arnav opted to try his hand at whaling on a whim. After a lengthy career at sea as either a navy man or a fisherman therein he required an even greater challenge with his beloved once more.

Having survived the War of 1812, he didn't feel too keen on returning to combat and fishing is a constant competition with other men that was somewhat tiring him. But why not hunt even bigger fish so to speak?

This dilemma once encountered, he easily settled, when signing his name to a four-year expedition onboard the British whaler, *Windlass,* out of a port in the Carolinas that had just returned from the ample grounds of Greenland.

Never did he feel such cold than on the voyage around the Horn and that of arctic winds even though a summer had duly arrived when sailing the narrow passage between Alaska and Siberia. The chill of that air is such that it enforces slumber in the fetal position like that of a hibernating animal. His dream of that wearisome journey began from a day, in his bunk, and frozen all over.

"Show a leg, Sailor!"

"Aye, aye."

Arnav rose intolerably, hitting his head on the bulkhead and dressing himself with all items lined mainly with otter fur and composed of sealskin. The second mate liked to jest with Arnav, for, of course, Arnav was no ordinary sailor but certainly not a whaler yet.

Nevertheless, Connor Arnav was made third mate for all

his experience and dignified composure. Neither man felt quite awake yet, but both heard the joyous hollering on deck. "Be there whales off the starboard bow?"

"Aye, that be my guess from what I can hear."

The second mate was a dear companion of his and once a 'twenty-pounder.' Otherwise known as persons under indentured servitude. A harsh Scotsman, David McMillin spent a straight seven years of his life hoeing and hauling tobacco on the plantations.

He got his contract at an opportune time in life, for the prices of 'twenty-pounders' skyrocketed, as did the demand for labor. A willing participant in the trade, as he was, became a rare occurrence. In the States, alas, African slaves have come to replace the practice now of late.

Under his 'apprenticeship,' McMillin became a wealthy man, but only fighters such as he can endure such contracts. Before our dreamer stood memory of a man with much fortitude and one accustomed to a life of harsh labor. That's where whaling came into the complexity of his life's work. Arnav and McMillin alike were born true campaigners for a life of toil and strife, as had most all whalemen.

The latter's hide, charred even tanner than the prior's, was profoundly scarred, for, alas, the man was ginger-headed. In his stares, one could see the soil he toiled for ages on - dust permanently buried deep into his face. Arnav respected McMillin, for the man was a Highlander, born and raised, and not a lowland-transplant like himself.

SUMMER ROSE PECK

"ALL HANDS ON DECK!"
"DROP THE ANCHOR!"

Together they readied themselves, racing topside, and grinned when they saw whales breaching in the ice fields upon the stark, choppy swells of the Chukchi Sea. When lowering away, a captain's mate would stand at the head of each longboat of which there were three.

McMillin would descend first with his chief harpooneer, McPherson would follow second with his, and Arnav third. On this day, Arnav occupied the third armed with his own lance since his chief harpooneer took ill with scurvy.

Captain Horner watched over his men fondly from the upper deck as a king on a balcony overlooking his subjects. Yet a superstitious fear seemed to be writ in his face at the sun, which remained fixed in the sky. It shone blood red and was secreted by violet clouds over an arctic desert that, as of now, his men reigned victorious over.

The crew advanced upon an enormous beast and past glacial boulders rowing and singing after their quarry like madmen. With a song and a bloodlust in their hearts, it wasn't long until they punctured the mighty predator's hump with their lances.

A great bloodbath ensued, which stained the pure white fields. The ice was red, the water was red, and even the snow itself turned red when it fell from the sky and into pools of the whale's blood.

THE MERCHANT & MARINA

On that day, Arnav pitched his first harpoon and struck a right whale for McMillin had taught him well. The crew, winsome, hauled their prize, and treacherously, through the snow-spotted sea, leaving behind a grisly scene.

For only a few minutes, Arnav stood with nothing to do upon a forsaken terrain watching his breath fly away. "A blood-red sun magnified like a sheet of glass watching over this gory scene. How portentous," thought he and all the while trying to remember how frighteningly bleak the environment appeared before returning to *Windlass* to take apart his first whale upon a bay of the North Bering Sea.

Slaying, tugging, and securing the carcass of an animal such as this was highly unpleasant but enjoyable if one could appreciate the fine process of the stripping without spewing. The stench would grow more and more foul as the hours wore on, but oh! There was something rewarding to this work, gruesome though it was.

With a crew, at least with these men anyhow there was unity in the backbreaking labor. Everyone sang together, worked together, ate together, and above all were miserable together. Whatever animosity the men held against each other; none cherished an offense for too long a time.

They either handled disputes by bickering it out in floods of obscenities or fought it out like men. That would serve a double purpose by settling an argument and providing the wearied crew with some sporting entertainment before being flogged for insubordination.

Unfortunately, this was a rare luxury since no questions were asked about a man's reasons for going to sea. That is unless they offered it themselves. No man ventures out to sea without a past and no doubt, a handful aboard were convicts and thieves. There is nothing like this kind of hard labor to set a man straight from whatever disease of the mind they may have.

Once a whale was hauled and strapped onto the icy hull, Arnav would oversee the tonguers cut up their pungent prize plentiful with oil, bone, and blubber. Never did he forget how dreadfully the wind whistled in their ears as they did so and how bitterly cold the gusts were too.

Never did he forget how uncannily the metallic clatter from their tools, pics, and axes resonated from the lee side and throughout the desolate terrain.

The *Windlass* sheathed with ice from bow to stern stood stiff and proud. The trips made to and from her never ceased, for the sun never set over this barren wasteland, and not even once a day came to an end.

Several hunts to slaughter the elephant seals would commence likewise for their oil and thus the seals for their fur. But always to the sea, they'd return to hunt the mightiest creatures of the sea and livelier in new hides.

Ages would be spent in that biting atmosphere until barrels upon barrels of oil were filled to *Windlass'* keel, and the dreadful stench of whales became their own.

Then on would they sail south for Tahiti with full stores

and an entire crew overjoyed to feel the temperatures climb. Subsequently, that month would prove to be an arduous price for warmer weather.

Storms tossed *Windlass* endlessly until the crew felt they could bear it no more. Ultimately, and off the coast of Guatemala, the gales broke off most like a fever over twilight seas. On one such evening, McMillin rested in the masthead, reading many a tale of love and loss and hate and lust when he met a horrid end.

Had Arnav, McPherson, and Captain Horner not beheld it with their own eyes, they would have never believed it when a bolt of lightning struck and killed their dear second mate cooped aloft. It terrified all on board, and many believed it bode ill.

At sea, a sudden stroke of lightning can appear to have no origin. Their deadly arms reach for the ocean's surface but retract in a flash as though they were never there, to begin with, and illuminate night like day.

All hands, even the fearless, would clap their ears at God's wrath and hide below from His resounding thunder. None risked venturing on deck for some time after McMillin was struck and fell into the depths.

A series of the doldrums set in daily following their crewmate's eerie demise and unhappiness. A sensation, which followed them ever since they left the arctic.

To the surprise of the men, no events of any significance transpired while on course and making berth several more times in South America, aside from the usual restocking of provisions and the making of repairs. They stuck to their course and arrived safely in Tahiti in the year 1827.

For sure, Arnav believed the Caribbean intensely beautiful and the Mediterranean tranquil, but those places were nothing to him compared with the glory of the Pacific. He discovered how sinful the Pacific Islands were, either reigned over by bloodthirsty cannibals or friendly hosts.

On the isle of Tahiti, one could indulge in any pleasure they wished for the sun always shined, the skies always remained powder blue, the birds always sang their sweet tunes, the seas swayed calm and clear, and the women were eager to soothe a sailors' pains. He never wanted to leave Tahiti, for it was their coconut fronds, kind faces, and Narita that whisked him away from all his miseries...

It had been so long since he had dreamed so vividly. Whenever images such as these in the night came, they were soon over and replaced with violent memories. Yet that night, they lasted and lasted. This dream was the kind you desperately seek once awake but can never seem to return to, no matter how hard you shut your eyes.

"Hector... I wanted to see the Cape of Good Hope."

Arnav groaned while the dog licked his face, but the dirt brown mongrel pranced about happily and barked, pleased that his provider was still alive.

"Ugh, my head…" he whispered, cradling his forehead, and easing out of slumber. Our merchant captain rose from his bunk, startled. Carefully he examined the waters swaying idle and less choppy than yesternight.

"Nay, I must of, dreamed her. I must have, but she seemed so real," pondered he. "Marina, she said her name was… Marina. Surely I could not have dreamed that up."

Stumbling from the bunk, he rushed to his desk and ransacked it, dust flying. Documents of all kinds he kept buried in its shelves, including ones from *Exodus*.

All sorts of trifles, trinkets, and nautical contrivances graced his home. A substantially sized marlin mounted one wall, and collections of scrimshaw, fishing lures, and nautilus shells sat idly on his many shelves. The sea chest that lay retired by the desk went with him on every voyage ever made under his Captaincy, and his name was etched gorgeously into its woodwork.

"Damn, if only I still had my log… Ah-ha!"

A certain sadness fell upon him as he found a flyer, once written to discover Marina's identity and notify her family. "This is so poorly written," he realized sitting, down and petting the dog. "I am certainly no writer, Hector, but at least my heart was in it."

Copies of this he hung in ports of Ireland, England, and Scotland, but no one ever came forward to name his flighty damsel.

SUMMER ROSE PECK

ATTENTION

On the twenty-fifth night of May 1840, a young woman was lost to the Atlantic on a crossing to New York. The migrant girl was a stowaway and the first casualty I ever received under my command. Her identity to I, and my ship's company, remains unknown. If possible, I sincerely hope to notify her family of her passing. I would also like to learn the young lady's name so that I might pray for her eternal soul. These were her physical characteristics.

About 20 years of age
Brown hair
Over five feet, lean
Blue/Green eyes
European-like facial features

> *My sincerest condolences,*
> *Captain Connor Arnav*
> *Commanding Officer of the American*
> *merchant vessel, USS Exodus*

Few merchants ever went through such measures over a lost passenger, especially a migrant. Many, however, allowed filthy conditions for their passengers and gleefully plied the lash to stowaways. Oftentimes such conditions were not even fit for animals.

"I wonder why she would brave such perils all by herself. I wonder why she fled Britain to risk sickness, hunger pangs, and Atlantic tempests. She must have indeed been quite desperate. There be more to it than that, though. This 'spirit' came to me for a reason. Perhaps she was an orphan once, same as I."

"Marina…Marina," he repeated aloud. "Lost on the twenty-fifth night of May. That was indeed five years ago last night. Either my mind is brilliant, or I really did see her Hector, whatever she is. A ghost, an angel, a demon perhaps… but as a-a fish that I cannot reconcile. You saw her, did you not, boy?"

The man looked down at the dog, who beamed at him as always. "What should I do, Hector?"

As though he understood his master's problem, the dog led Arnav over to the edge of the dock, where he snorted at the deck boards. There he discovered Marina's tarpon-like scales. Some wedged in the wood, which were the size of silver dollars.

"My God," Arnav knelt slow and examined one closely. "It wasn't an alcohol-induced hallucination or some reverie. It was real. She was real. Unless they are just that, the scales of a tarpon…"

CHAPTER SIX

THE HUNT

The sun was rarely seen nowadays in St. John's County, hidden behind grim plumes. Hector proudly sauntered by his master's side as the man walked past the gray fortifications of Castillo de San Marcos. "This fort has stood for almost two hundred years..." Arnav reflected while the dog roamed past him. "And yet is still impenetrable."

Castillo de San Marcos was built by the Spanish in the late 17th century and took over two decades to complete. Now in 1845, Arnav ambled by the fort in awe as it stood proudly on the shores of Matanzas's Bay and undefeated by time.

THE MERCHANT & MARINA

"People can prattle on about the west all they want, but this place, now a state rightfully belonging to the Union, is indeed bizarre," thought he in awe.

"Such a strange region and one that possesses immense weight in history. It is said this is where Ponce de Leon first landed the *Santiago* in his infamous search for a fountain whose waters grant life. He is the one who gave this place a name meaning 'full of flowers'…"

Sea creatures covered Florida's shores, and beasts both beautiful and terrible thrived inland. Unique races constantly fought for dominance of this marshy kingdom: the native Seminole tribes, the Spanish, the colonists from the north, the Cuban refugees, immigrants, etc. Arnav knew of one Englishman that lived nearby, but he doubted there were any other British men in the whole territory.

"I wonder just how many mermaids if there really be any, dwell deep beneath the surface of the seas," Arnav began to ponder. "Perhaps they hide in nearby coves and reefs. Could they have townships, cities, and kingdoms, like humans? Do they live in pods like the dolphins?" Indeed, many strange questions came to mind.

"But she's dead," he remembered. "She would be a-a mystical being of some kind…" and again, our merchant captain recalled her curious words…

'For men of the sea and those lost to it, the sea has reserved its own heaven and hell…'

The skies though heavily clouded, were quite warm and the humidity overwhelming. Arnav strolled with his coat open, allowing his white undershirt to flow freely and in a most piratical manner.

"Hector!"

With a whistle, he called forth the dog who had found a playmate by the fort. Hector answered his master's beck and call, obediently though hesitant to leave a new friend. Patting the dog's head, Arnav stood before the seawall and gazed over calm waters.

"Marina said she would return to me at eight bells, but apparently, my eyes and senses cannot be completely trusted after dark. I must discover what she is."

Connor Arnav concluded what any sensible man of the sea would about a fish, that he was to catch her.

Back in the boathouse, Arnav prepared the *Seminole* to make way, and his conscience arrested him a while at the thought of bringing along a lance. "I cannot harm Marina, but what if she is indeed dangerous?"

Some seamen believe that mermaids are God's creatures; fortunate and fair undersea beauties obligated to save sailors from damnation in Davy Jones's Locker. Others say they are the spawn of the devil. In conclusion, seductive and evil tricksters designed to drag all seafaring men down into an abyss with an alluring melody.

"Both may be true, I suppose," was his assumption and wavered between the slip and the dinghy. At this time, he remembered the Irish equivalent to 'merfolk.'

The mythical creatures known to the isles as 'selkies.' Maidens, who supposedly, in the forms of seals, shed their skin once on dry land to reveal a human woman.

"Perish the thought. After all the clubbing I did in the Arctic, I certainly hope that's not true…"

Arnav sat for a moment happily disgusted with his seamanlike sense of humor and grunted, "in all seriousness, this decision I make could mean the difference between life or death."

Arnav pulled a line, allowing the dinghy to float into the sea, and raised the sail. The dog stood on the bow, enlivened. Hector loved to assist his master and thought this mermaid hunt no different than any other fishing trip.

The harpoon, he left behind but brought a pistol that rested comfortably in his waistbelt. All his usual fishing equipment lay neat at the bottom of the *Seminole*, including his largest net.

Today was eerie, and the bay remained deserted. He noticed some fishing off the docks and local urchins playing on the island; their little sailboats wedged in the sand, but he saw no man else in a boat.

"Alas, fishing season isn't till June. Hopefully, Marina will move on by then, granting that I do not catch her."

Sailing past the brush of Conch Island and into the

waters of the Atlantic, he felt foolish. The midday sky grew darker and darker, and Anastasia's lighthouse shrank with every glance astern. Ominous and steadfast, the *Seminole* rocked stiffly upon the open waves.

Even now, the weather was mild but, in this region, storms could appear out of nowhere, especially when clouds such as these covered the sea. "Are the currents rough, or is it just mine eyes that make them so?"

Every once and awhile, the halyards upon the rigging rustled, and Hector grew disturbed. It is apparent that dogs cannot speak as you or I do, but they communicate and clearly with soulful stares. Arnav translated the mongrel's eyeful warnings with ease.

"Beware the skies, Master. They do not bode well ..."

Resting on the tiller, he sighed, "perhaps this venture is ill-timed," while staring at Hector, whose cries began to annoy him. "Hector, stow it..."

Soon the dog's whimpers became an alarming bark, and Arnav saw a glimmer of silver pass beneath the *Seminole*. "It cannot be," thought he but firmly gripped the net and waited. As of now, he didn't have the patience to set up a line and try to hook her. "Nay, she may be too smart for that anyhow..."

Apprehension grew in the man as his weight stood suspended over an uneven sea and balancing on a swaying craft. "What I saw last night was most certainly a drunken delirium. Why am I going through such dramatic efforts to secure my own fantasies?"

But aloud, he pronounced his firm resolution, condemning all reason. "Mermaid or not, whatever just swam beneath us, Hector is massive, and I'll be damned if I do not catch it!"

Breaching from the starboard, Marina revealed herself to Arnav in the light of day, and he could not believe his eyes. "My God, you are real... A true siren of flesh and blood!"

A frightening glare engulfed the beauty of her eyes, and pure ire made them gleam.

"Does she have powers beyond my comprehension?" he began to fear, and the distress showed plainly in his face. "Could she actually consume me as easily as a barracuda or a shark would?"

"Thou art hunting me, Connor Arnav!"

"Aye, damned right I be!" he shouted with some relief at still being whole. "I am haunted by a great many things, and I do not need you stirring my soul unto madness!"

With that sentiment, Arnav hurled the net over Marina into the sea. The sky instantly turned black as he did so, and thunder rolled. Hector cried even louder, frightened at nature's sudden transition from calm to tempestuous. In a tight grasp, he held the net but could not find Marina.

Arnav braced himself, and believing that the mermaid had alluded him, he resorted to his pistol. Not even he knew why he had reached for the weapon. Anger engulfed and overwhelmed him, no different than the sensation of drowning. Pistol in hand, he pointed it towards the sea, prepared to fire at the first glimpse of silvery scales.

Below, Marina evaded the net, and with one hefty thrust, bashed her powerful fluke against the keel.

The blow threw Arnav off the dinghy like a ragdoll, and he powerless to prevent himself from being knocked over. No crests formed on the seas, but its surface swayed violently and drove floods of white water over his head.

"Hector! Hector!" he cried.

Coughing and spitting seawater, he called out for him again, more worried about the dog's safety than even his own. The animal had likewise been thrown from the *Seminole* and remained unseen, but the man heard his cries aft of the derelict dinghy.

Arnav swam towards the *Seminole* in long strokes, and his sturdy arms and legs began to weaken against the forceful swells. Mustering the strength, which he knew was somewhere within him, Arnav hoisted himself alongside *Seminole's* hull and slumped over, but the ocean was vengeful and guided the drifting net into his path.

Beyond the craft, Arnav saw the dog struggling to paddle in his direction and urged him on. "That's it, Boy! C'mon! C'mon, Hector, you can do it!"

But that furious and rapid swell thrust the net round the man's legs heavily. Arnav frantically searched for his knife on the shipboards to no avail before the weight dragged him down. Thrashing, he fought to stay above the rageful waters.

All the while, the small craft, derelict reeled helplessly with no commander at the tiller, and Arnav failed to elude. The bow struck him, and he sank beneath the waves, still conscious with both hands bracing his wounded head.

Nature treated him to a great show of lightning on the surface. The thunder's clamor stayed muffled beneath the waves which burst above him like clouds of snow. The crushing fathoms were cold and black.

Much of his life blazed before his sorrowful eyes, whilst a shanty, one he loved and recently heard played in the tavern, seemed to be sung by whaling angels.

It's a damned tough life full of toil and strife we whaler-men undergo…
And we don't give a damn when the gale is done how hard the winds did blow…
For, we're homeward bound from the arctic ground with a good ship taut and free…
And we don't give a damn when we drink our rum with the girls of old Maui…

Still, the man sank deeper. The cold Wilmington streets that raised him did not surface in his visions. The visualizations seen were only of times at sea. Just as in his dreams again, he saw the beautiful Pacific islands on crystal waters that were close to Heaven.

Rolling down to old Maui me boys...
Rolling down to old Maui...
We're homeward bound from the Arctic ground...
Rolling down to old Maui...

Still, he sank deeper. The countless occasions he spent listening to Captain Lange's stories during their lessons on *Gallant* first came to mind. The images could have made him weep had he not been engulfed.

However, some sights were disturbing and came in violent flashes, such as the horrors he witnessed on *Magister*. Just as a bolt of lightning had struck and killed his crewmate cooped in the masthead of the once-beloved whaler *Windlass*, the sight struck him too.

Perhaps the memory most pleasant was when he played tag with Narita on the white seashores of Tahiti. The *Windlass*, lying at anchor in the bay and Narita's raven-sheened hair flying as she sprinted before him in the sand.

The last sight, not even known to be had, was that of Marina admiring him while boarding *Exodus*. For only one moment in time, she had once locked eyes with his, and evoked his passions.

On that morning in May, Marina caught Arnav's fancy with her stares, and he remembered his infatuation.

THE MERCHANT & MARINA

"How could I not remember that face at first sight? The one whom I knew in that instant was my one and only love. How fleeting the glances, I returned to her were on that Spring day. How oblivious I was."

With a dainty hand placed on her chest to secure a scarf, he recalled how her eyes fell to her frocks and then to the boarding planks amongst a flock of Irishwomen.

Water charged down his lungs as his eyes rolled and shut. Had they been open, he would have seen Marina. Her angelic silhouette outlined by streaks of light on the surface with his knife firmly gripped in her hand and majestically plunging under the great pressure of mad fluxes to rescue him like a dove swooping down from on high.

Rolling down to old Maui me boys!
Rolling down to old Maui!
We're homeward bound from the arctic ground!
Rolling down to old Maui...

CHAPTER SEVEN

THE

TAVERN

He felt the slight drizzle of raindrops, the grains of sand under his hands, and heard the ocean swish while coming to. Unsteadily he rose, allowing one hand to support an aching head. "Tis true what the sailors say of the sea being much like a woman," thought he aloud. "No matter how much she hurts me, no matter how angry she becomes, I still love her. Blast, my head hurts something awful…"

Twisting about, he observed his boathouse, still standing as decrepit as always. Arnav felt relieved to be ashore upon the treasured sands of his own beach again but instantly remembered the dog. "Hector…"

The man promptly got to his feet and scanned the beach for his beloved animal. "Hector! Hector! HECTOR!"

The *Seminole* was nearby, beached and overturned, and his equipment lay scattered in the sands, but they were not a priority. Skinning his eyes, the merchant captain realized just how much he took that dog for granted.

Hector was his only companion, family member, and crewmate anymore. A deep self-loathing seeped into him at the loss of such a helpless animal, whose responsibility was his to protect.

Sadness was not a feeling new to Arnav, but this was a special kind of despair that touched his ravaged soul.

When you fail another human being, they have a capacity to understand your faults and forgive your mistakes. A dog, for the most part, depends on a human master for their livelihood.

The horizon remained stark gray, which did nothing to elevate his low spirits. "I should ship again," he realized and with much difficulty.

"I am only forty-seven, and yet I act as though I were an old man and even old men go shipping. I do not think I can bear to be alone anymore," sighed our merchant captain glaring over the woeful waters.

"I must return to the merchant service. I want a crew and a ship again. Perhaps I need someone to go home to at the end of my voyages. Marina," he said her name aloud. "She's why I gave up shipping and relinquished command of my brig to Mason. A position not so easily surrendered too. Now she may be the reason why I return to the sea. What a shame I could not have created a life with her. She saved me, but why? Seeing as I failed to save her." Then he sighed, "I wonder where my beloved *Exodus* be now."

For hours, deep thoughts came as Arnav searched for Hector up and down Matanzas' Bay. His hopes wailed with each passing minute of not seeing that mangy face. The only consolation he found was in the thought that perhaps the dog was stranded on Anastasia.

Nevertheless, in the late afternoon, he finally gave in. Staggering, he collected his equipment, making several trips back and forth from the shack.

For such an ugly day, the sunset bore intense hues which the Atlantic reflected like a mirror. Brilliant bright blues, purples, and pink patches of light were lashed together by silver clouds that blanketed the golden sun. Every form was shadowed and drawn by the shades.

As the sun set over the horizon, at last, it came time to haul the *Seminole* closer to the boathouse. Wearisome, Arnav decided to make repairs on her at first light.

He felt determined to search the inlets for his dog the next day, even if it was a futile effort, and possibly go hunting to justify the search.

Our darkened merchant captain perceived a whimper

towards the beaten and battered *Seminole* and thought himself mad at first until he heard it yet again. "Hector?" Again, there was the slightest cry. "Hector?"

Arnav traced the sound to the dinghy's overturned hull and lifted the bow with both hands. "Hector! How in blue blazes did you get trapped under there?"

The dog emerged from out under the ship, uninjured and tail wagging madly at the sight of his master. Arnav embraced his pet, laughing as the last rays of sunlight shone upon them in the sand. Cheerfully, he thanked Heaven for his friend's safety but soon yearned for the tavern.

Upon arriving at Abelardo's and shuffling along the cobblestone road, his head throbbed painfully. Arnav stepped foot through the door and was greeted as warmly as always.

"Senor Arnav! You look terrible..." the taverner affectionately teased this notorious man of the sea. "What did you do today? Wrestle with a leviathan?"

"Thank ye, Abel. Nay, but it feels just so. Rum, please," he begged while sitting down to a table.

"Grog?"

"Aye, grog."

Arnav sank down for the last time today, and Hector laid beneath his master's boots sleepily whenever they made a long interlude here.

This establishment had the appeal of a home, and that indeed it was. Abelardo and his young wife, Maria, dwelled above their business with five children. Their affection towards each other could endure anything and was mainly fortified against poverty.

Arnav believed them to be the loveliest Cuban family in all of St. John's County.

Hector happened to be especially fond of Abelardo's children considering they paid him the most attention. Late at night, once they were asleep, the lady of the household became his favorite. The Senora often treated him with left over bones or anything else she could scrape up.

Many local, lonely seamen flocked to this tavern over others specifically for that familial atmosphere and Maria's beauty. To Arnav's relief, tonight, there were no crowds. The few men around him drank and spoke quietly between themselves. One grizzly-looking fisherman played on the accordion and half-asleep in a corner with a cap covering his sleepy gazes.

The air prevailed that night in salty breezes and could be tasted on the lips even while indoors. There is more oxygen by the sea, and our merchant captain breathed in the salt air heartily, for it was just another form of medicine to him. Calmly the lights flickered and were effective in dulling his senses.

Maria glided over to Arnav's table smiling, and her brown eyes were glad as well. The gold crucifix round her neck glistened in the candle lights, and her scarlet skirts made pleasing ruffle sounds as she walked.

The taverner treated his wife like royalty, and it always showed in her dainty face. Nothing made this woman happier than her children and working beside her husband to serve spirits to sailors - the simple pleasures in life. Abelardo was by no means a wealthy man, but Arnav thought him incredibly rich.

Charming and kind, Maria treated her customers with the same attentiveness that she would give to her own sons. "Senor Arnav, it is so good to see you again," she spoke while placing a mug on the table. "I had a feeling you would come in tonight. The skies have been so gloomy late- Dios Mio, what happened to your head?"

"Oh, it's nothing, Senora. I threw some iodine on it."

"This is not nothing," she examined him and repeated his words mumbling, "threw some iodine on it..." in reproval. "Abelardo!"

The taverner knew he was in trouble for something and sauntered over.

"Abelardo, are you just going to let one of our finest customers sit here with a gash in his head?"

"No, not now," he laughed with a sense of guilt. "Forgive me, mi Amor. I did not notice."

"Bring me some dressings, por favor."

"That is not necessary, Senora," Arnav insisted and feeling flattered. "I am quite alright."

"You sit still right where you are, Senor Arnav," she commanded and fetched water. "That wound needs to be cleaned and dressed."

Arnav could never disobey the lady of this household out of pure affection. He abided her sweet commands, although uncomfortable with the growing audience. Her husband brought over the proper dressings as she gently cleaned his wound. Abelardo found amusement in everything and most often in his wife's overly mothering nature.

"Oh, Maria, you are fussing over him," the taverner laughed while placing a fist on his hip in observation. "I am sure Senor Arnav can handle a little cut such as that."

"Is that gash what you consider a little cut?"

Maria tapped her tongue and shook her head at her husband. "How men can manage to take care of themselves without a woman around is beyond me."

Again, the taverner bellowed with laughter. "So, how did this 'grave injury' happen, Senor?"

"Well, um, I was fishing, and a sudden swell threw me off my feet-ah," Arnav lied and took a swig.

"Sit still."

"Yes, Ma'am. Anyhow, I must have hit my head on the mast. Fortunately, when I came to, I hadn't drifted too far."

"Did you catch anything?"

A faint smile crept upon Arnav's chin as he replied "no," and gazed down into his mug. "No," he simply muttered once more.

Abelardo returned to his work and Maria seemed pleased with hers. "There, is that too tight?"

"Oh no, it is fine. Muchas gracias, Senora."

"Senor Arnav," she plead and wrung her hands. "Will you promise to keep the bandage on?"

"I promise, Senora, and thank ye again."

Caressing the dog, Maria reached into her apron and pulled out a bone for him. Hector readily accepted her gift, and she hurried to serve the human customers who were in the middle of a spirited debate on pirates.

"And I say piracy is criminal by its very nature, Senor," spoke a gentleman at a table. "All of their practices are sinful."

Arnav hadn't yet seen the face of the older man at the bar counter to whom the Spaniard addressed, but he listened in, quite interested.

"I grant that most pirates was violent killers they were and aye thieves, but not me dad. Many of em' were just lookin' for freedom from oppressive government they were, and rightly so."

"Ah, the infamous lone Englishman of Florida," Arnav believed. One could see how short he was, perched on the stool like a buzzard. The old man seemed intrigued by piracy with a childlike fascination, topped with a tricorn hat and draped in a long buttoned-down coat in all.

Our haunted merchant captain decided that there was something innocent and kind about his cockney voice and straggly white hairs.

"Me father, he was a pirate," he chuckled and drank. "I suppose that be whys I defends them sometimes. No prey, no pay, he used to say!"

The Spaniard at the table grew uninterested, but Arnav was still curious and spoke with a tone free of accusation or judgement. "Did he tell you much about his life on Caribbean seas?"

"Nay, he ne'er got the chance," the old man answered and excited at the stranger's interest.

"They hung him when I was no more than ten years old, they did. At no other than the infamous 'execution dock' in London. It was 1792 it was."

Arnav knew he would sorely regret his following words but spoke anyway with great distaste at his own stupidity.

"Did he ever tell you any lore about sea creatures?"

"Oh, all sorts!"

"What about um, sirens? Or mermaids?"

The taverner led the men in laughter and snickered, "why have you seen any lately, Senor Arnav?"

They mused and laughed heartily, but the old man was quiet and knew that Arnav questioned him with sincerity based on his tone.

"Oh, belay that, gentlemen," the old man growled. "Stow it!'

"Well, I don't rightly remembers him much, Sir, but he did use to tell me all kinds of sea lore and such tales. Matter of fact he did tell me a belief amongst his fellow blighters 'bout mermaids once. Let's see, what was it?"

The old man searched his thoughts carefully, scratching his head, and drank a little to help the thinking process.

"Oh! Nows I remember."

"'Danny, Lad,' he says to me. 'Mermaids are the spirits of women drowned at sea whose souls just simply cannot rest...' Especially, the ones who went to their watery graves terribly like being thrown overboard."

"Why would a man throw a woman off a ship?" the Spaniard inquired aloud and in a virtuous manner.

"It be bad luck to have em' on board, that's why!"

"I should think having a woman on board to be of good fortune," a man at another table jested.

"Nonsense!"

The buzzard's feathers were thoroughly ruffled now, and he fidgeted on the stool. "That rightly proves you're not a sailor. Sailors used to throw em' overboard because that was so, especially pirates."

"Well," stammered the gentleman conceding to the elder. "A man would have to come from an awful kind of lot to do such a thing."

With that observation, a chair in the establishment abruptly scraped against the floorboards, interrupting the peaceful atmosphere.

"Are you going home already, Senor Arnav?" Maria kindly asked our shaken merchant captain.

"Aye, I'd best be shoving off now," he mumbled and placed the proper payment on the table. Maria noticed his hands tremble as he did so.

"It was nice speaking with you, Sir," the old Englishman spoke and raised a glass to Arnav in parting. "Are you from Edenborough by any chance, my good man?"

"Nay, I was raised in North Carolina," he answered, buttoning his coat and fumbling. Again, Maria saw Arnav struggle and came to assist him for only moment. She felt concerned over his nerves, which seemed quite shattered.

"Wilmington is notorious for their flocks of Scottish migrants," he laughed very tense and tried to act naturally.

"Well, anyways, it always be a great pleasure to meet a Scotsman! What's your name, son?"

He pronounced his calling proud, "Connor Arnav."

"Captain Connor Arnav," Maria clarified from a distance serving more tavern dwellers.

"Senor Arnav used to be the captain of a merchant vessel," explained the taverner in a complimentary tone, which was rare for the seldom serious man. "Now, he provides the town with the finest catches."

"He's the best fisherman in St. Augustine," Maria added braggingly with a perky chin. "And he used to be a whaler."

"Well, I don't know about that, Maria," Arnav smirked humbly in response to his new title. "But thank ye."

"He has been all over the world!"

"Ah, it just so happens that so have I! You must then

truly be a man of the sea, Sir! My, my what a career. I don't suppose you were old enough to serve in the war, Captain?"

"Eighteen twelve?"

Arnav froze at the inquiry but answered truthfully. "Well, aye, I did. I served as a ship's boy in the United States Navy during the second war for independence. It was a hell of a way to mature."

"I served in the Royal Navy," the Englishman replied with pride and shame in his words, which surprised Arnav. "I hope you won't hold that against me, Sir! I would like very much to meet with you again and hear more about your time at sea from one sailor to another."

Again, the old Englishman raised his mug and smiled, revealing little to no teeth. Arnav smiled as well and felt as if an old wound had just been healed.

"Well, I am always here. Abel can attest to that," he said, slapping the taverner's shoulder in farewell. "Next time, we'll speak further and drink together."

He paused, realizing that he didn't catch the old man's name. "Oh, I neglected to get your name, Sir."

"I'm Danny," he said happily at having found a kind new friend and one who was not afeared by his many years.

"Midshipman Daniel Brown as I was once known."

"God keep you, Mr. Brown."

"And you, Captain Arnav!"

Arnav gave Maria a respectful kiss upon her dove soft cheek in gratitude for her thoughtfulness and generosity.

"Many thanks to you again, lass, and bless ye."

Then with a nod of his head, he ushered for the dog to join him and left the establishment. "Come on, Hector. It's time to go home now. Come along, me bucko."

Once the two were gone, Maria spun around to face her husband, announcing, "he's far too lonely, Abelardo!" with both hands on her hips. "You need to find him a wife!"

"Well, mi Amor," the taverner hollered, "it would have to be senorita who loves the smell of fish!"

CHAPTER EIGHT

THE SURRENDER

That evening never blackened against the stars but only glowed a darker blue as the night wore on. Basking in the moon and lanternlight, Arnav paced the rickety deck boards on the outer slip of his boathouse. Silently he hummed a shanty and whispered the words awaiting midnight.

"We'll rant and we'll roar like true British sailors
We'll rant and we'll roar all o'er the salt seas
Until we strike soundings in the channel of old England
From Ushant to Scilly tis thirty-five leagues…"

SUMMER ROSE PECK

Generally, he swore off the tune '*Spanish Ladies.*' The song reminded him far too often of the 'redcoats,' but tonight, the shanty refused to leave him. The stars seemed to enjoy it too, for they danced and glistened, and some streaked the sky. Subtle winds rolled over in their sleep and made the palms rustle.

The waters waltzed with the nightly breeze, and the crickets served as their orchestra. Fireflies flickered, floating amongst the groves, and glowed in the same dim light the lanterns did. Again, the bells rang eight, but he did not mark it.

Ding, Ding
Ding, Ding
Ding, Ding
Ding, Ding

"We hove our ship to, with the wind at sou'west boys
We hove our ship, deep soundings to take-"

His formidable voice stuttered with a note of despair, and another, far prettier voice carried on the rest of the lyrics for him.

"'Twas forty-five fathoms, with a white sandy bottom
So, we squared our main yard and up channel did make."

THE MERCHANT & MARINA

"Marina…"

"Thy shanty be off-key, Captain," said she in a corner that edged towards the sea and lifting herself onto the deck. The mermaid smiled dearly at him, in a playful manner, and seemingly proud of her heroism.

Rays of moonlight magnified the iridescence of her tail as sunlight through a diamond. The fluke, hidden beneath the water, shifted, rarely seen. As always, Marina's face was fair and made even more beautiful by the lantern light, which assisted him in noticing one or two scales beneath her eyes. Those tarpon-like scales blinded Arnav at times and gleamed brighter than the comets. Her arm hung o'er her head as she lay against the rail, catlike.

"You saved me, Marina."

The canine sat beside the mermaid, unafraid of his rescuer, and gently she stroked him.

"Not yet I haven't… and it will not be I who saves thee. I can only show thee the way."

"Who then?"

"Thou knowest the answer. Search thyself for it," answered she and trailed off examining the bandage round his head. "I see thy wound has been tended to."

"Aye and I apologize to thee- you Marina," expressed he regretfully and shuffling his hands on the rail. "I did not mean to harm you."

Her brow rose quite unconvinced. "Oh?"

"I cannot believe that I almost shot her," he remembered

with a frown. "I wonder if she knows that..."

"Aye, and I mean it sincerely."

"I shall forgive thee," she said but noticed the firearm strapped to his waist. "But only until thou removest thy 'blunderbuss'..."

Arnav glanced down and slowly removed his pistol, hesitant to surrender it and surprised that he managed to secure it before his plunge.

"I must a be damned fool," he thought while fingering the weapon and eyed Marina for confirmation. "Ah, the powder is probably still wet anyways."

With great reluctance, Arnav laid the pistol carefully on a barrel behind him, and she watched him do so with the focus of a feline. "As I told you a'fore, I am haunted by a great many things."

"The unjustified execution of thy crewmates."

Connor Arnav threw his head back violently in response to her statement. "Why must you remind me of that accursed day? Why must you haunt and torture me? When will you let me be?!" Our merchant captain seemed in a great deal of pain though nothing physical ailed him.

"I could have saved them," he stammered, unable to contain it any longer and racing fingers through his umber hairs. "I could have saved them all!"

"Thou wert only a boy, Connor Arnav. What wouldst thou have done?"

"Avenge them! Avenge them at least!"

THE MERCHANT & MARINA

Arnav paced the deck again, sorrowfully, and could not look at Marina any longer. To him, she appeared nothing more than a symbol of his greatest fears and failures hidden behind a form only he would recognize, a fabled creature of oceanic lore. "Vengeance rarely has the desired effect one thinks it will," was her stern reply.

"I've found myself upon a lee shore. I do not understand what evil compels men to commit such crimes."

"Of course, ye know not," Marina argued and visibly appalled. "Thou must be evil thyself to know why. Yet even in life, I knew the purpose of pure men such as thee, and that is to vanquish evil."

"Then I failed even at that..."

Arnav collapsed on the edge, considerably closer to Marina than usual, and palmed his heavy forehead. "I failed to save them, and I failed to save you. Survival has a hefty price that I have learned from life."

"I have never envied or respected one that has not known struggles such as thou hast," she spoke with passion.

"Wisdom, humility, and strength are born through such brushes with evil. I shudder to imagine what kind of person thou wouldst have been without the contest to win. Do you fear me?"

"What?"

"Dost, thou fear me, Connor Arnav?"

"Nay," he whispered and taking some time to answer. "I suppose not. Not if Hector does not fear you."

Arnav fondled the dog as well and tried to reach her hand through Hector's fur. Since Marina was lost, it would be the first time their hands touched, and he sorely wondered how it would feel to hold hands with a spirit.

"Does blood still run through her veins? Perhaps I am about to find out."

The mermaid gently placed her hand upon his bandaged wound without invitation and mumbled something that he could not hear. Her caresses and compassionate eyes comforted him just as they had the dog though he was sorely baffled as to how.

This close, she did not appear to have veins as he assumed. There were none on her arms, yet there was warmth to her touch.

"Wait- how could I not have noticed those before?"

Glancing over her again, he was mystified even further at the bits of shine, which dangled from her ears. "Where did you get those?"

Marina wore earrings suited for royalty. Earrings that she fondled, smiling shy when Arnav inquired about them. She even appeared to blush a little. How that was possible, he hadn't an idea.

"Dost, thou like them?"

"Aye, indeed, I do."

"I found them today."

"Are they pure gold?"

It was not the mere fact that a mermaid wore earrings

that perplexed him but their immaculate design. Marina trusted Arnav well enough, and so she allowed him to take a closer look at her treasure in the dim light.

"Nay, they cannot be real, but they certainly look real." Her earrings hung woven in the tint of gold. They were subtle but quite impressive. From the gilded cords on each ear hung a tiny dark jewel that glinted green with every flick of her head.

"Emeralds!" he declared aloud and unable to restrain his enthusiasm. "Actual emeralds and gold, my God! Where did you find them, Marina? They must be worth a small fortune! Did you salvage them from a sunken galleon? From the Spanish treasure fleet?!"

"Oh, Connor Arnav, allow me to show thee marvels," entreated she with delight and disregarding his frantic plea for clarification about her jewelry.

"Marvels that will make thee, most glad to have survived. The sea is what stirs thy soul and drives thee on, yet thou hast only voyaged across its surface. Thou hast ne'er seen what beauty lies beneath."

"Lovely words," sighed he thoughtfully, "lovely words. If only I knew what they meant."

Often, Arnav felt bewildered by Marina's quaker-like speech, and all he heard just now was the word 'beneath.'

Marking the silent fear in his face, she clarified her good intentions with a giggle. "Nay, I shall not drown thee, Connor Arnav, I promise! I thought thou wouldst trust me by now."

Trust is a feeling more fraught with betrayal than any other. This Arnav understood and feared greatly. Yet, at one point or another in life, trust is necessary and, if utilized well, can be an instrument to achieve true happiness and possibly, under these circumstances, Spanish treasure.

"What hast thou to lose now?"

Thoughtfully and silently, aloud, he asked, "what must I do, Marina?"

"Place thy hand in mine. Thou shalt breath water as naturally as thee taketh in air."

Marina lowered herself into the water and bobbed when her weight went into the sea with a hand outstretched to Arnav. Beheld within those sage eyes was such an innocence that the merchant captain could not refuse. Yet he also noted the innocence of the worried brown eyes which sat beside him.

"How long?"

"A day, Captain," calmly answered she. "One day at sea as none other living has seen it before."

"Nay... Nay, I will not go!"

This he declared in panic and suddenly thought himself a fool to even consider such an insane proposition.

"How does one breathe in water without drowning?" he pondered frantically. "Granted, Marina does, but she's dead after all."

The mermaid looked upon Arnav fearfully at his sudden

outburst and withdrew her hand.

"I will not go ye hear! Tis true you mean to drag me under. If so, I do not know why it is you felt the need to save me. Perhaps you want the pleasure of drowning me whilst I am still conscious!"

"Twas not devil's work or evil tidings that brought I to thee but providence, Connor Arnav."

"Bilge!"

"Then thou didst lie in saying that thee trusted me."

The merchant captain rearmed himself, clutching and brandishing his pistol in the air. "Why did you ask me to surrender my firearm unless you were planning to do something that I would shoot you for?!"

"I would never harm thee, Captain."

Silently Marina bobbed, and with a frown, she bid him farewell. "Tis a shame, thou canst say the same to me… Listen to me carefully, Connor Arnav," sighed the mermaid with tears falling from her eyes.

"I cannot take thee on this journey against thy will. Thou must come with me of thy own accord and without fear. Mine offer expires today. If thou wouldst only accept, ye may knoweth what is it to be joyous again. But if not, then thou must be content in drowning thy sorrows away with liquor forever."

"Marina… wait…"

"Dost thou not, remember the way thee used to be? The way thee used to be so long ago before the world had corrupted thee so?"

"Marina…"

Alas, it was too late. The mermaid returned to her underwater realm, fluke slapping against the surface, and Arnav doubted that he would ever see her again if not for her bidding remark.

"'Mine offer expires today,'" quoted he. "Surely then I shall see her by the 'morrow. I hope, I dearly pray."

Arnav rose early that morning and anxious. Sometime during the night, the pain in his head had grown so intense that eventually, he passed out again. For our merchant captain, it was customary to wake with headaches but never had he been awakened by them.

Staggering to a mirror, he splashed some fresh water on his face and ripped off the bandage, startled to see no injury. Traces of the gash, now sealed, vanished by some miracle. Not a single mark nor a tinge of pain remained.

It had been so long since his mind felt this clear and light. His eyes seemed alive for once, glaring into his reflection, and his limbs felt sturdy enough to search for Marina once more.

"What a fleeting feeling, especially at daybreak this be. The bulk of my thoughts tends to weigh me down each day but not this morning. If I find Marina, I must thank her kindly for her blessing."

THE MERCHANT & MARINA

Not long did he have to go in searching for his mermaid when he shoved the door open and stumbled onto the planks. Marina lay in the sands before him, amongst the surf and in broad daylight. For the first time in weeks, the skies were bright, and the sunshine no longer concealed by the clouds.

Such a pure sight this was. Hector sunbathed on the captain's crude porch and heartily chewed on one of his many bones from a private collection. The animal appeared comfortable with Marina's presence. No longer did he ward her off with barks, nor did he growl.

Dressed in the same attire from yesternight, Arnav did not bother to bring a coat or hat to shield his face from the sun. Again, he was clad in the same white buttoned-down shirt and naval blue trousers but removed his black leather knee-high boots and left them on the porch with Hector.

Captain Arnav marched through the sand barefooted and proud, for it was the only way he knew to walk.

Evidently, our sailor had given in, casually slumping into the gentle surf beside the mermaid. Only out of the corner of his eye did he observe her while scanning over the waters - his arms resting upon his knees and fiddling with a piece of driftwood.

Arnav could not recollect when last he saw such a beautiful and colorful day. The brush, the skies, and the seas were the colors they should be. Not gray but green, blue, and even more blue. "Aye... what a bonny day and beside such a bonny lassie."

Marina's tail angled over her back, and the fluke hung o'er her head like a ladies' parasol. Such was the intricacy and detail on her tail that could never be seen on any tarpon unless you were lucky enough to snag a massive one.

The scales shifted with every twitch and flex of a muscle, and her fluke was indeed massive. It was more substantial than he could have ever imagined, and he felt overwhelmed to see it this close. She sparked the intrigue of the fisherman in him, which was the very voice he wished to silence in her presence. "Her fluke is about three feet wide; I believe. I wonder how much she weighs…" pondered he so intently that he did not even hear her words.

"Art thou still frightened of me?"

"Perchance she weighed about one hundred and fifteen to one hundred and twenty in life. I estimate the tail's weight alone to be at least sixty. Combined, let's see that would be -"

"Captain Arnav?"

"Oh, hm? Oh, my apologies, Marina. My mind was someplace else."

"So, I see… Art thou still frightened of me?"

Arnav gave no answer, only his hand.

"I see thee art prepared then," said she with purity and a grin. "Come."

Marina shifted deeper and deeper into the surf and urged him to follow. Stomping through the water Arnav did not

THE MERCHANT & MARINA

feel like an animal falling into a trap. That afforded him some ease. Seldom did his instincts ever fail him.

The dog watched his master's departure from the beach and seemed content, for he soon scampered through the sea-green groves without care. The stride towards Marina seemed so long an effort, and the water fought his march.

Waist deep into the translucent green waters, he took her hand accordingly while she placed another on his chest.

"Hold fast to my hand, and this time, do try not to let go for thy sake more than mine."

Tumbling beneath the surface and caught in her wake, Arnav panicked as she pulled him under, feeling horribly betrayed. Marina would not release his hand, and so he thrashed like a fish on a hook to free himself.

But the water was her element, and in it, she was much stronger than he. Marina took Arnav's face to hers, allowing him to perceive the kindness in her eyes. The captain's breath-hold, longer than most, persevered, and he steadied himself a while to read her face.

He waved his hands up to force himself down and blew air from his nose to sink even lower. In and out, Marina expelled bubbles, encouraging him to inhale ocean water but persistent was he in his refusal.

Though gentle, the waves upon the surface rocked them from side to side between land and sea. Each sway carried towards the sands, but Marina defied the current's power.

Her eyes softly shut as she leaned in close to give him a

gift, a legendary mermaid's kiss. The bubbles blew and burst, racing to the top like sparklers.

Carefully Arnav permitted some seawater as she pressed lips against his and ideally came to the realization that by some miraculous grace, Marina was allowing him to breath in her world. The smile on their faces could match no others as sunlight shone through the reflections dancing on the surface.

CHAPTER NINE

THE ANGEL

Looming above came a great beast of fantastic proportions, a striped monster with soulless black eyes and a jagged smile. The tiger shark seemed to pass Arnav and Marina, lurking around them in one long circle, while they knelt on the bottom motionless. She weighed her companion down, and he gripped her hand tighter and tighter with every aggressive shift of the creature's tail.

The tiger shark could only implement one eye, which transitioned from black to white instantly with every blink. The other eye was gone, leaving behind a caving scar. Bottom dwellers hid beneath the sand and permits bowed their ugly heads in reverence at his approach. This formidable predator appeared preoccupied and only curious about the mermaid and the merchant captain who continued forth on their journey once out of his sight.

"What ecstasy to traverse and breathe in the blood of the Earth!" thought the captain ever so joyfully.

"I no longer feel the scorching of the sun's rays, only the warmth of the watery atmosphere. Light pierces through the surface and forces the hides of every living thing to glisten in harmony."

Clusters of fish of all dimensions and hues glided past, projecting their shadows on the oceans' surface in lively sways. Some were menacing and generous in length, others only minuscule minnows.

Yet all were vivid and colorful as though their radiant bodies were composed of nothing but precious metals such as silver, bronze, and gold.

Surfacing on a sand bar past the inlet, the ocean appeared to be as smooth as the buffed side of a gem, a gem that transitioned from emerald to sapphire with every length they traveled. Catching his breath on the sands, Arnav jested about their harrowing rendezvous with the fearsome and phantom-like tiger of the sea.

"I have only seen them from above, never below," he laughed, breathless and exhilarated.

"They seem a lot less frightening that way, only majestic. How remarkable that their stripes should gleam underwater and those rows of razors! I do not believe my heart has ever beat so fast!"

Marina sat upon her fluke and ran slender fingers through her lengthy umber hairs.

"And there is still so much more to see. Still yet so many perils to encounter. The ocean tis the blood of the Earth pumping life all around us-"

The captain noticed her sentence abruptly cease, her eyes caught on the horizon, and a benevolent smile formed on her countenance.

"What is it?"

"Quickly, come with me!"

Marina rapidly plunged into the surf, and Arnav crashed in after her. She briefly emerged from out of the white assault and caught him in a hug instead of stealing him by the hand. Gliding through the waters, Arnav marveled at the rate in which she now swam, regardless of his added weight. Her fluke propelled them with the velocity of a sailfish and went with such a swiftness only to be found in nature. Further and further, the distance grew between himself and the bottom of the sandy globe.

"Everything lives, even the water itself has a pulse. There is no gravity, and my mind carries no weight. Sound resonates superbly in my ears and all my senses tingle. This awareness of everything around terrifies me and yet excites me beyond belief."

Surges of sunlight spun just as she did through the blue

surface and with every variation made. Her hair waved up and down and side to side just as groves of seaweed with the currents' motions. She smiled at him then stared straight on ahead. 'Look…' she seemed to say.

"My God, I have never seen the like…"

Before them, shot a pod of dolphins playing tag and flying through the water effortlessly as birds on a breath of wind. Happily, they chased one another and embraced their brethren with such love and devotion. All their movements teemed with a passion for life.

"I - I have never seen them this way before."

They appeared to be playing games like the sorts you would see humans throw on an Easter Sunday at church and the merchant captain dearly wished to join them. Marina released Arnav cautiously but still held his hand firmly to guide him even nearer to the playful creatures.

Our merchant captain was happy to be underwater, else ways he would be seen wiping away tears of joy. Dolphins have always been a symbol of good fortune to sailors.

Never did he see a more majestic sight than that of porpoises leaping out of a tall ship's wake under the sun or with trillions of stars to guide their way.

However, many appeared uncertain about the newcomers interfering with their familial gaiety and remained vigilant. The speckled elders were wary and knew far better than to approach such peculiar beings.

They tended to keep their distance, but the younger ones

were curious about these strange and mysterious forms. One knew Marina and zoomed in to play with his old companion. She placed a palm on his nose delicately, and he sped in circles taking her along with him.

Once freed, the aquatic dancer held onto a dorsal, and her partner lifted her through the seas.

Arnav held out both hands when one swam close, but the suspicious juvenile immediately changed his mind and whirled away. Again, he held out his palms and patiently when another swam nearby. This one seemed calmer and friendlier though very shy.

"Probably a female," he believed in awe. "She's so little and so lovely. Her eyes are just as sweet and innocent as Hector's." She alone inquired an elder's permission first.

The dolphin rested her bottle-like nose in Arnav's hands, and he treasured the touch of her steely-soft skin.

"Such incredibly sleek proportions! Such lines they have, and these elongated tails have the capacity to take them anyplace on the watery globe. How I envy them."

The merchant captain marveled at this display of trust from his new friend and beamed just as bright as Marina did back at him with pure bliss.

However, her lover soon grew jealous and whisked her away from Arnav, who still floated there, amused.

"Beneath the surface of the waves, all my heartaches seem to sink and only leave my uplifted soul. Such energy these porpoises possess! And I already begin to tire."

To and from the dolphins soared past, but the merchant captain could not keep up with them by the mere stroke of his arms and politely ushered for Marina's aid. Merrily, she took him in a hug again, and they joined the lively pod.

"I count at least a dozen. How powerful they must be to ward off stormy seas and cut through the currents like the atmosphere itself. How tough their skin must be to resist such cold as the Atlantic possesses in certain seasons. Marina must be just as resilient to match their pace even with the added burden of my weight."

The dolphins charged towards the surface like a herd of Poseidon's steeds, and the merchant and Marina followed, matching their quick pace. The waters echoed sharper near the surface, and the deafening vibration consumed Arnav's ears. Every sound hammered him, for the dolphins' shrill dialect was just as overwhelming as the stifled sounds of waves battling above.

The travelers were enveloped by the current the dolphins created in stampeding across the surface, and now Marina swam amongst them with ease. Their unified momentum carried her as they reeled speedily along. She held Arnav with both arms across his chest to allow him to see the majesty of these Atlantic stallions.

Before them, the fiercest of the pod violently hurled themselves out of the sea and plunged back in, impaling the surface with their noses.

Now that guests were present, they felt obliged and

thought it only proper to give them a show. Their sharp fins and flukes slewed the oncoming impact of the waters, and they appeared to laugh in contempt at the oceans' pitiful attempt to slow their pace.

Cutting through the undercurrents with this pod of dolphins was more intense and more beautiful than any sight imaginable.

Arnav's smile stretched from ear to ear, and Marina was glad too. Yet even she began to grow weary and soon removed herself from the momentous energy of the pod.

Gracefully the two sank, and the sea above grew quiet and still as the dolphins charged on without destinations or courses to trouble them.

Once more, they rested upon the shores of a Floridian inlet and for some time. Arnav caught his breath while lying in the ample shade beneath a palm listening to winds sway over his face and the waves creeping onto the sands.

Marina sat on the bulk of that same palm which angled over the waters majestically like an outstretched arm.

Her silvery fluke dangled into the clear sea with both eyes bonded to the horizon. She seemed to be scanning for something across the distance: something else besides the sun which shone so brightly above and searching for something beyond the glistening sphere.

Her lengthy hairs blew with the wind, but she was in

some meditative state and did not move with them.

"Who are you, Marina?"

Arnav stood behind her now, and she acknowledged his question with a turn of her chin over a shoulder. She seemed willing to answer and gestured for him to sit beside her on the palm.

"I would tell you more about my past," he said, awaiting a reply and mounting the trunk. "But something tells me you already know everything there is to know."

Arnav hesitated, for he had so many questions to ask of her that it was difficult for him to think of them all at once.

"From where did you come? Are you British?"

"Yes, I was English."

Marina answered him decisively and with a special emphasis on the word 'was.' To avoid looking at him directly, she leaned over, plucking a starfish from the water, and cradled her precious find.

"How old were you when you – when you-"

"Thou meanest when I died."

"Aye," answered he and with a great note of reflection resounding in his voice.

"I was nearly twenty-four. I also had some Irish and Dutch ancestry in me, too, by the way."

Arnav felt that last remark explained at least a few things about her nature and her facial features.

"Why did you make the journey, Marina? Why did you not pay a fare? Were you penniless? Were you alone?"

"I once had a great many pennies to my name," she told him despairingly. "But alas, when I chose to board *Exodus*, I had none, and yes, I was alone. More alone than I had ever felt in my entire life."

"Who were your people?"

Arnav hung upon every word she spoke now, thoroughly captivated by her life's story.

"My family was quite wealthy but not financially speaking by any means. We had enough to live comfortably, but I always felt rich because of them."

Marina saw the confusion in Arnav's eyes. "My parents," she quickly clarified.

"My parents... I lost them both over a period of three years. My father first, then my mother. I think that it is when I truly died. I was their only child. Yet, they were not even my birth parents. Rather, an older couple from the county of Yorkshire, who, quite lonely, took me into their home when I was very young. I was an orphan once, Connor Arnav same as thee."

"They sound wonderful, Marina. I always wanted such persons in my life. You were fortunate to have them."

"I always thought so," she stated sadly but proud. "I should think my adoptive father would have liked thee a great deal. He always wanted to be a sailorman despite a game leg. He was a veterinary who nursed all manner of animals, especially horses."

Marina giggled in thinking upon what were undoubtedly

fond memories.

"Oftentimes, I would sleep with more than four or five stray dogs in my bed. I suppose that is why I adore thy 'Hector' so well… All of us, dogs and all would visit my extended relatives in Ireland every spring, in Castleknock. My uncle was a landlord, and his wife, my aunt, a refined Irish lady. They were quite wealthy and their home immaculate. I loved them dearly," she sighed with much longing and seemed to be piecing their faces together now.

"I assumed that they would take me in when I needed them, and they did but eventually attached strings."

"What do you mean?"

"My aunt and uncle made ultimatums and conditions to my living with them after a while," Marina explained. "They threatened to disown me and turn me out of their home unless I agreed to go to school."

Still, she held the starfish tenderly in the palm of one hand as would a child embracing a doll.

"Twas not that I disliked learning new things or felt ungrateful. In hindsight, perhaps I should have expressed more gratitude for their offer to send me to school. Very few girls are so fortunate, especially with the current conditions."

"Maybe," she stuttered. "Maybe I should have braved the storm, but I'm not sure dying was much worse. School always seemed no different than a prison to me. I generally taught myself anything I needed to know and immersed myself in the studies that I felt passionate about. I do believe that I would have been quite content as a scullery maid for the rest of my days just so as long as I had a book in my hand."

Marina sighed in reminiscing and adjusted her seat on the palm, as did Arnav.

"This certainly would have been a first for the sorts of passengers I had," he discerned without conviction. "A migrant escaping wealth."

"For a time, I considered going to the convent to become a nun so they wouldn't send me away, but all I ever wanted out of life was a family. It seemed like such a simple desire at the time and one that they would admire having so many children themselves but not without a formal education, I suppose." Again, Marina fiddled with the sea star.

"They were quite eccentric and believed that all young ladies must be educated in the most monotonous of studies, deportment, chiefly amongst them. I had to be taught etiquette and become fluent in French and Latin. Such intricacies were incredibly difficult for me to learn. I did rather enjoy the piano, though I played it terribly."

Marina attempted to smile and seemingly mask some inner woe. Her throat tightened, and her voice quivered whilst finishing her unhappy tale.

"Oh, Captain, they expected so much from me, but I was dearly afraid of disappointing them. I do not understand how people so wealthy could have been so poor in my eyes!

Not once did I ever run away from my parents' hovel, but I did flee from that stunning mansion. I bolted out of my uncle's house like a spooked mare one day and to the shipyards of Dublin just as fleetly as my legs would carry me. I shan't burden thee with the rest, Captain."

After hearing her story, Arnav now understood why she had fled from him and his officers. "She was so young and spirited and eager for adventure. I was just as foolish," the merchant recalled and smiled.

"The sea liberated you and I both," he seemed to say with a fleeting glance. "Though in one way very separate and more tragic than another. We're alike in so many ways, Marina."

His head sank, and she muttered, "but then I saw thee," becoming a little happier.

"I saw thee standing on the deck of thy vessel so proud and free, the sails billowing in the wind. That is why I stole passage aboard *Exodus*. I trusted thy looks. I knew thou couldst take me to the New World, safe and sound. For a month, I went unnoticed and stole food from the galley."

"I would not have sent ye back, Marina, and for a litany of reasons, the first being logistics," he grinned, aiming to get her to smile again too, but she would not.

"I know that now. Do not blame thyself for my loss, Connor Arnav. Twas my own fault…"

Arnav took both her hands in his and felt great sympathy for her. "I would have worshipped the ground she walked upon," knew he with much disappointment. To him, there was something so naturally attractive about this spirit. He saw an inner light that shone about her eyes of peace, love, and forgiveness. "Perhaps that is a luxury which comes in the end. It is apparent that in life, she could have never harbored hatred towards anyone."

Even in death, Marina's face was innocent, and yet that same somber face seemed so mature without being decked in rouge.

"But now I have a holy purpose, Captain," she raised her head and finally revealed a timid smile. "And one in which I must perform well to be reunited with those I dearly love."

"To help me?"

"Aye, Connor Arnav."

"I do not understand. Are there more," he mumbled. "Are there more like you, Marina?"

"Yes," was her grim reply. "All poor souls lost to the sea, now one with the deep...."

Again, Arnav had countless inquiries as to the divine mysteries of the sea but was frightened of the answers he'd receive now. "'For men of the sea and those lost to it, the ocean hath reserved its own heaven and hell,'" he thought, quoting, and cursed in considering the whole phenomenon.

"Oh, to hell with it."

Based on her tone, he believed that strange remark to be the only answer he'd ever receive on the subject.

"There are many things I cannot share with thee, Captain," she spoke unexpectedly.

"But dost thee know the feeling when half asleep and a kiss grazes a cheek, but no one is there? Or when strolling down a street, how the wind calls out thy name, and the leaves follow ye along the way? Or what about when thee goest by the seaside where that same sensation lingers, and the waters seem to welcome one with open arms?"

"Aye," he replied, suspending his feet above the water, and maintaining balance. "I believe I do."

"Cherish these simple things that make ye feel alive and be grateful for them. Heed them the way you would a superstition that bodes ill or well at sea."

As much as Arnav took to heart the bewildering advice, he could not help but mutter a question that had been on his mind for years. Therefore, he furthered his inquest.

"I once wrote a notice, Marina, regarding your identity. I hung copies at several ports in Ireland, and hell, even in England and Scotland. Did not your wealthy Irish family ever go searching for you?"

"That I cannot answer, but I do know they were not the sort to ever be caught frequenting the docks. I am sure they did seek me out, however. My aunt and uncle cared for me even though their ways of demonstrating love were foreign to me."

Marina noticed Arnav's face go long. He knew her pain profoundly and brought it upon himself. There's many a man with the vice of thinking too much or too little. This rugged old salt of a sailor knew himself to be an overly empathetic man and thought on things with more passion than most. It was a strength of his just as much as it was a grave weakness.

Sorely, he wished for another kiss but knew it not the proper time to ask for such a delightful remedy. A remedy certainly effective in treating thoughtful afflictions.

"Do not be sad for me, Connor Arnav."

The mermaid gave the merchant a peck on the cheek and half on the lip as if she knew his utmost desires.

"I am free. Now... come with me."

Arnav grinned content even with a modest kiss from this angel of the sea. From the palm, she lowered herself into the sea and freed her reddish, five-legged friend.

"Where to next?"

"A very special place and hidden," the mermaid answered briefly and fiddled with her earrings. "I only hope I remember where it is."

CHAPTER TEN

THE GALLEON

Marina and Arnav submerged leisurely now over a vast coral reef where the surface loomed far above. The sun bore down upon vibrant corals that spread all over like an underwater meadow. An underwater meadow painted and swarming with life in every form.

"I feel mesmerized by these pigments so vivid and bright. My eyes cannot take in all the hues at once."

For him, the brilliant tones stirred memories of the tropical blooms on Tahiti. Rays of light frolicked over red, orange, and purple arms that felt coarse or even stung to the touch.

THE MERCHANT & MARINA

As with all things Marina showed him beneath the seas, he had only ever seen such miracles from above.

On the surface, he has gazed upon countless reefs all over the globe. He has glided above the ranges of the Great Barrier Reef, which extend over the coral seas, the endless crusted lengths of Barbados, the colorful ridges strewn across Pacific islands, and hidden deep within the Caribbean, but this was not the same.

From below, the corals were not treacherous, multicolored hazards to navigation but dwellings that secreted all varieties of marine creatures. Unless they swarmed beside one another in shoals, none of these marine critters were quite alike.

Some wore stripes like the tiger shark, but many were adorned with speckles or even spots to distinguish themselves. Above, tuna flew by in silvery hurricanes, and hordes of mahi charged past.

Crimson crabs crawled stealthily on the bottom amongst many shells, and emerald eels poked their heads out every once and while to find food. A pair of war-torn lobsters battled for territory and fought to no end. The mighty claws of one component evenly matched another.

Some steel-backed stingrays glided over to see the visitors in their aquatic kingdom and sneered. An octopus sped nearby and hid, for he was shy in the presence of newcomers. The fish all stalked one another, and none were ever quite at ease.

From out of their hideaway, a pair of minnows emerged to greet Marina, and what a magical sight it was. They zoomed about her like puppies but retreated into their hollow once they saw she brought a companion along.

Giggling, she bade her tiny friends goodbye with a wave of her fluke. The mermaid was just another local to them and one worthy of affection, for she provided protection from bigger fish.

Marina halted Arnav to scoop up some sand from the bottom and opened her hand to present him with a scallop. She tore the two interlocked shells open with minimal effort, revealing the flesh inside. Implementing two fingers, she pried out the meat and ate it raw. Then with a smile, urged him to pry another open and try it.

Scallops were an oceanic dish that he never tried raw, and so he too dug one up, sand flying, and cracked it open. Mouthing the meat, he found scallops in their natural state to be salty and delectable, though a slick texture.

This outing on the reef reminded him of a day in his youth when he took a young lady out to the orchards to pick apples and snickered at how incomparable it was to this.

With the mermaid by his side, he collected a few more scallops to sustain himself along the way, not realizing how hungry he had become.

As the rays went over the corals, so did they, too, ripple across Marina's scales, causing them to shine in waves with every sway. Still, Arnav inhaled water but knew that once this ended, he'd forget how it felt entirely. Therefore, he savored every inexplicable breath taken and the tranquil state in which he found himself beneath the sea.

On they went hand in hand, through an aquatic tunnel created by nature and past the reef where all the exquisite colors began to fade.

In 1715 a great hurricane swooped over southeastern Florida, and the mighty Spanish fleet was driven into the coast on course home from Havana and the vanquished New World. Heaven punished the conquistador's greed by sending their pilfered plunder down to the deep.

Upon that fateful day, the Santa Cristo de San Roman fouled on the edge of a reef, and her wreck emerged before our travelers in murky waters ahead, towering. Yet, of course, only one out of the pair knew the name of the galleon conquered by the seas' elements.

Her shadowy figure bore down upon them like a specter, and her severed ribs lay spread on the bottom. An eerie vision this ghost ship was, and it sent tingles rushing up and down Arnav's spine. He shivered as the waters instantly felt colder at the haunting sight.

Sharks circled the desolate wreck endlessly charting and recharting new courses, projecting their fearsome shadows on the sandy bottom. Marina gave the sharks a wide berth and alluded their fearsome silhouettes this time. She knew them to be rather unpredictable creatures and quite territorial, especially in groups such as these. Arnav understood that one taste could lead to a feeding frenzy but remained calm and swam slowly.

"For one hundred and thirty years, she has rested here and has not seen the true light of day since. What a violent storm it must have been to have sent such a majestic vessel under and how overloaded with bullion. Her foundered sisters must indeed lay nearby. Dear God, a galleon..." our merchant captain muttered mindfully.

"A real-life galleon. I have only seen them in books. I bet her might was unrivaled by any other naval force in the world. I doubt even the Brits had such imposing warships as this one undoubtedly was."

Marina came broadside of the hull, slowly raising and lowering her fluke in long strokes, allowing Arnav to see the damage amidships.

The galleon's hull was punctured from the hard formations below and the mainmast had clearly fallen from powerful gales, for it lay mangled over the port bow. The fore and mizzenmast were gone completely either removed by winds or swells.

No doubt, they lay strewn someplace and broken amongst the many other beams wedged on the bottom. Her royal-looking forecastle and multi-leveled stern castle were dissolved by time. They were essentially the ruins of what was once a floating fortress.

THE MERCHANT & MARINA

The bowsprit still stood firm, forever imprisoned by the surrounding formations. She groaned as the depths weighed heavily on her rotting timbers. To Arnav, the moaning of a ship, be it underwater or above, always seemed alive and caused him even greater uneasiness.

Claimed by the reef, her labyrinth was now home to the sharks, barnacles, and crustaceans crawling all over. Marina drew Arnav further down and beneath the fallen mast until they gazed into the blackness of her injured portside. With an apprehensive glance, Arnav appeared to ask, 'are we going to enter?'

Marina knew the inquiry behind his looks and nodded. Above, the merchant captain noted the sun only as a point of light glistening on the surface.

Through the opening they entered, and into the galleon's hold intended for ballast. Nothing could be seen, for the surroundings were pitch black, but Marina seemed to know where to go with Arnav's hand still safely placed in hers.

Bulkheads above and below and from all sides, creaked which alarmed him in addition to having his vision temporarily deprived.

The waters remained dark until they rounded a passageway where the sun shone directly through an overhead hatch extending all the way up to the main deck.

Gliding into the blue-tinted light, they found themselves passing through the lower deck packed to her keel with ghastly-looking barrels of supplies and stores.

Silverware and broken China sat everywhere; the pieces scattered about. Still, all he could perceive were the figures in the shadows and thought at times he'd see a conquistador's ghost hidden in the corner of his every gaze.

Higher they drifted in a hug, and every level became brighter upper decks. Upon reaching the gun deck melded with the last two levels above, Arnav wished to explore it, and Marina abided him.

"These were the heaviest guns of the vessel, and many still lay intact!" he observed with boyish glee. "How I do wish to have sailed on a galleon!"

Marina appeared worried by the enthusiasm writ on his face, and her looks urged caution. Arnav noticed this and raised both hands in a motion that said, 'I promise not to touch anything.'

He meant it too. The last thing he wanted was for the whole wreck to buckle on a pressure point and be forever entombed by her broken limbs. Carefully Arnav glided towards the 'canones' and 'culebrinas' entirely rusted over and examined them only with his eyes.

In staring upon the artillery, one with an imagination could almost hear their pummeling blasts and the shouting of Spanish voices which commanded them. Those mindful sounds faded away like ghostly reverberations passing through his ears.

On the main deck, remnants of a time long forgotten and worn away by salty currents waited to be uncovered.

THE MERCHANT & MARINA

The only armaments left fixed to the deck were by mechanisms likewise engulfed by sea life. Towards the stern, Marina led him through a tight opening of what little remained of the captain's cabin.

She entered first, persistent that he should follow, but Arnav hesitated as he did so. Enclosed by darkness and timber, he grew alarmed. The passage stifled him, and after several feet, he couldn't move any longer out of terror.

Marina swam ahead with ease, flicking her silvery fins, and disappeared. He lost sight of her entirely down the narrow tunnel. Once he did try to move again, he found himself jammed.

For moments, which felt like hours, Arnav resisted the urge to panic, and from out of nowhere, a hand clutched his wrist. Marina had returned and slid down the passageway in reverse with both hands gently pulling him free.

The light, which pierced through the dark, intensified as he emerged from the tunnel and found himself in the captain's quarters. Above, a small skylight allowed him to see the cabin.

"How stately these quarters were. The construction must have come from Cuban lumber."

Although crumbling and misshapen the furniture was clearly elaborate and constructed well. A massive desk centered the cabin, and the bulkheads were paneled, carved with the most ornate of patterns now green.

The bunk he assumed at one time was swathed in the

most lavish of crimson cloths. Three grand portholes graced the stern of the cabin and were, mostly, still covered in a diamond pattern providing even more light.

Neither of them gave much heed when a shark or two would sweep by the stained and mostly shattered glass.

Gently he picked up a weapon lying on the charts not yet entirely rusted and examined it with great solemnity.

The Spanish long sword clutched in his right hand stirred feelings of grandeur and a love for the ways of old. Its cruciform hilt, inlaid with silver bullion, still retained its intricacy, and the blade was double-sided. Humbly he laid down the weapon right where he had found it in reverence to whomever once captained this fine vessel. Even this weapon he knew would have been considered a relic in its owner's time.

"What stories it could tell…"

A small chest all at once caught his eye on the shipboards beside the desk, and Marina noticed. Connor Arnav was not a man of greed, but, if possible, he wished to take a single silver peso in remembrance of this day.

For all three years that he has called St. Augustine home, never did he fail to skin his eyes for the faintest gold or silver shimmer combing the sands. Around town, it was believed that treasure from the 1715 fleet could be found washed ashore, but Arnav certainly didn't know of anyone so fortunate.

He was loath to lay a hand on the chest, but Marina

drifted over and opened it carelessly. She pointed to her earrings then back at the chest to indicate their origin.

"Oh, so this is where you found them," he said only with a raised brow and heartfelt smile. She merely mouthed the words, 'look inside.' At first glance, the chest once lined with felt appeared empty until he looked in deeper.

Being motionless, Arnav began to float, and Marina helped him down each time he did. Almost a dozen coins lay contained within the chest, and all silver, save only one. She gave him a slight nod and encouraged him to take it. Reaching a hand into the chest, he removed a single coin almost two inches in diameter and gazed at the mermaid in gratitude. With a happy grin, he examined his very own gold 'escudo' and safely pocketed it.

Now came time to leave this watery crypt, and instead of going through the tunnel, Marina urged him to push through the wood on the skylight already broken down.

It broke free with one pounding, but a barnacle secreted inside cut the palm of Arnav's left hand. Marina's jaw dropped at the amount of blood that rose from the injury and quickly tore off his shirt sleeve.

He would have already done so, but one hand was busy keeping blood in. She tied it around his wound as tight as possible, but the sharks now circled above the skylight like sea vultures.

CHAPTER ELEVEN

THE SUNSET

Blood rose in plumes. It was an exceptionally bad cut and poorly timed. They were trapped, or at least our merchant captain was. The predators would never bother the mermaid, yet she remained fearful. Fearful only for him. There was no way out other than the tunnel, which Marina dragged Arnav away from.

She knew the beasts would only be waiting for him on the end, and if left unguarded, they would flood in through the skylight. "Better to see the danger than not. Better to die fighting than be trapped on both sides. The skylight's my only chance."

Lower and lower the aquatic vultures swooped down,

and Arnav weighed his options to no avail. Eyeing the sword, he realized he wasn't unarmed after all. Marina had the same idea and retrieved it for him in a sweeping motion.

She handed him the weapon, but he was cautious in receiving it. "Nay, it'll surely fall apart in my hand if I try to use it, but what other choice do I have?"

With a firm grip and a sudden surge of bravery, he shot through the skylight halfway to fight his stalkers but could not find them. Badly now, he wished for an owl's vision. Above and below, he scanned his surroundings, restless, but the phantoms were nowhere to be seen.

Uneasily he fingered the hilt with one good hand and waited, staring into the distance. Shadows appeared and reappeared in that great expanse, and it became difficult to discern them from reflections.

The hull groaned louder, which startled him, but Marina still waited below the skylight to hold him in place. She steadied him without fail and patted his leg in a way that suggested encouraging words.

'Do not fear. Focus and relax.'

He felt just as though he were a fish in the reef, never at ease knowing that predators are everywhere and nowhere. Hidden and in plain sight. Maintaining a clear eye, he shifted his head from side to side and all around incessantly like a madman until he saw remnants of the helm.

It struck something inside of him. He couldn't take his eyes off the place where the ship's wheel once was. It threw him into a kind of trance, and once again, he heard the shouting of Spanish voices, but this time they did not come from his mind.

An immense shadow emerged from his peripheral vision, and he faltered to meet his first aggressor. Quickly he sank down for cover, facing Marina in cabin, and rose again without hesitation. He learned his lesson and took preparation for the next joust.

"The eyes on these creatures glow most demon-like," he discovered with the first tournament and grasped the hilt. His heart pounded against his chest, and sought, refuge someplace safer.

Another beast lunged in manifesting by magic, and our merchant captain readied himself. Again, Arnav raised his sword to meet the foe but missed. The shark flew by and on no different than a predatory bird.

Determined to slaughter an enemy, he raised the weapon once more when the first came in for another round. Arnav swung the sword and gloriously slew the oncoming beast creating a crimson cloud. His stalkers all swarmed in and revealed themselves to feast upon their fallen ally.

Marina made haste and pulled Arnav out of the skylight beneath the shoulders. They fled from the shipwreck and further out to sea whilst the sharks fed upon the flesh of their brethren.

He could no longer see the bottom, only a blue abyss. They swam together for some time, and Arnav began to ponder their heading. He assumed Marina had a bearing in mind, for she kept eyes ahead and emanated confidence.

A vast watery desert presented itself stretching for thousands upon thousands of miles. An open ocean, which could carry a person to any place they desired to go in the world. A vessel of freedom in the bloodstream of the Earth, and they only, two cells bound by sea and sky.

"Where could we possibly be heading," his mind raced to no end. "The Caribbean? The West Indies? To Africa or Europe, perhaps? Oh, if only I had me compass. How remarkable that would be and how perilous. Just Marina and I with the whole world at our fingertips."

"A day at sea, Captain. One day at sea as none other living has seen it before."

"But the day has almost ended now," he thought with disappointment in recalling her statement and frowned. "I suppose my skin would never last me such a journey anyways."

Arnav felt his hand sting painfully beneath the shirts' sleeve, which stayed wrapped tight around his hand and resting on Marina's back. That same intensity that had struck his head wound was in the process of mending his cut palm, or at least that was his theory for the time being.

A marlin shot by them at one point faster than a silver bullet. He seemed in a dreadful hurry and quite cavalier with his foil leading the way.

"What a fine catch he would have made..."

Aside from some sea turtles that swept overhead, blocking the crested sun, their path remained clear. All was silent and the sea windless above.

From below, a sharp melody resonated far throughout the endless stretch. It was a familiar pitch and one, which melded seamlessly with the great majesty of the sea.

"Whales," knew he instantly. "A whale's song."

Marina came to a halt and gestured with a swooping arm that seemed to proclaim, 'behold the largest marine creatures known to mankind.'

Four massive shadows emerged from the depths, and Arnav identified their distinctive outlines in awe. "Humpbacked whales."

Merrily the aquatic giants whistled and rose further and further to breach the surface before them. Marina released herself from the hug and calmly took Arnav's trembling hand, which shook out of exuberance, not fear.

She moved so gracefully through the water now, slowly, elegantly, and her fingers gently sloped like the hands of a ballerina performing an underwater dance. Every strand of brownish hair danced with her in unison.

There is nothing more powerful in nature's kingdom than the wake whales produce when surfacing. No other being could possess such energy as they. No other being could create a stronger current. These are the creatures that could stove a tall ship and send her under with one stroke of their mighty flukes.

Arnav felt convinced that even gales met their match when it came to these gods of the sea. The currents made by their tumbles thrust the travelers back and drew them forward all at once. Marina powered through the undulations, but Arnav had to implement every muscle in his body to defy the watery assault.

The family of four ascended and broke the glass-like surface, causing it to shatter into white water. A father, a mother, and two juveniles consisted of their small pod. Their barnacled gray hides told of many a tale without employing any language. On every precipice of their skin, the elders were scarred.

Those disfigurements told of intense battles with creatures unknown and unseen deep beneath the blackest depths of the sea. Arnav remembered when whaling how he'd see scars on dead whales not made by any human instrument, not lances, not knives, nor even axes.

"What monsters crawl and slither underneath the immense pressures of the abyss? Only the whales know."

They frolicked on the ocean's surface and sang sweet tunes in thunderous tenors. And here, Arnav thought the dolphins' lyrics far too loud! Just as a flurry of underwater snow, millions of bubbles rushed past when they approached the humpbacks.

From a safe distance, Marina introduced Arnav to her gigantic acquaintances with waves of arms and fins. Nearer they swam and our merchant captain sad at having once struck harpoons into the backs of their magnificent kind; woe at having torn apart their mutilated remains and stripping the bones bare.

"The deaths of their brethren serve a great purpose and for quite possibly millions of persons. At least now I can marvel without strategies in mind to slaughter them. Now I can finally appreciate the weight of their beauty. I do so love these creatures. How could I have ever butchered them? Aye perhaps, partially out of jealousy."

An elder came in the vicinity of the merchant and Marina and sung even more lovely melodies in greeting.

Upon closer inspection, she did not recognize Marina's friend and shifted her massive body allowing the traveler to see more of her. With a large kind eye, she examined our merchant captain.

Arnav now floated an arm's length away from her pectoral, and though unnerved, reached out to touch her. When feeling the tip of her fin, it felt as though he were connecting with an untapped source of power from mother nature. It humbled him but in a good sense.

The whales and their brood began to barrel roll and stretch, basking on the surface in what little sunlight remained. While swimming amongst them, Arnav felt honored to be included in their majesty.

He and the mermaid both twisted about just as they and playfully in the swells the offspring created when leaping out of the sea. To catch a breath of fresh air, Arnav rose to the surface and bobbed in dark waters.

There he observed the father's colossal fluke, perhaps the size of a sloop defined against the sunset. His tail towered over the sky and higher than the golden sun now so far across the horizon.

"Whenever I feel downhearted, I shall always remember this day," he vowed to himself mindfully. "Especially this moment."

As Arnav bobbed, he cheered and shook a fist in the sky out of exhilaration as the whale's fluke slapped against the surface before him, creating an immense wave. The force threw him under, and he smiled at the thrill.

The family of four descended and plunged deep, pulling the merchant and Marina along with them in their wake. The travelers allowed themselves to sink and followed the whales stealing as many glimpses as possible before the marine giants vanished below the depths.

Marina floated to the surface dragging Arnav by the hand to chart their next course. Towards the setting sun, they gazed, eyes full of radiance and marking every reddish shade in the sky. They plunged forward west and headfirst into the sapphire-tinted sea, bidding the last light of day goodbye, and perhaps for eternity.

CHAPTER TWELVE

THE FINALE

Sometime along the way home, Arnav fell asleep and woke to see trillions of stars against a black sky. He lay floating upon his back and breathed calmly in and out. His clothes were in complete tatters, but he did not care. Marina no longer held his hand, nor could he see her, and yet he felt her presence.

Therefore, Connor Arnav felt safe with every light stroke his hands made and felt at ease while resting upon the surface of the waters. Palms swayed with the nightly sea winds as he approached a sand bar on the inlet by his home. Just as he had imagined, the horrific tear in his hand miraculously mended on its own. Only old scars remained as he removed his improvised, bloodied bandage.

Beneath him, the sea glowed green as he swam atop what the sailors call 'green fire.' Floridian seas carry their own aurora borealis, so to speak, in currents rather than their atmosphere. Millions of organisms luminesced in waves all around and gave the surrounding sea a heartbeat.

Fireflies flew around pretending to be stars and our merchant captain having mistaken them for comets at first glance. If not for the alluring face which appeared out of the corner of his eye, he'd assume the sharks had returned for him. Marina swam broadside gracefully now, shifting her fluke from side to side in the manner a shark would.

The gray tip of her fluke sharply slew the tranquil surface. She hauled herself onto the sand bar first to lay on her back in the sand, and Arnav did the same.

Holding hands, they watched over the stars, which reflected off Marina's tail as always. In a single motion, he took her hand to his lips to give her a quick and tender gentleman's kiss. Quietly they listened to the serene waters rush back and forth with a gentle temper.

While lying there, they thought on many things which they did not share. Personally, he wondered just how many people looked to the stars before his time. He thought about all the marvels people who feared the sea missed each day and night.

"What are you, Marina?" he suddenly found the courage to ask and turned his head away from the brilliant skies.

"Will you tell me now? A ghost? An answer to a fleeting prayer of mine?" With the last question, he seemed to answer it himself by the way in which he spoke the words. "An angel?"

"What dost thou believe I am?" asked she mischievously with a thievish glance. After a moment, he merely replied, "the latter." The mermaid remained silent but smiled, nonetheless. Those oceanic eyes which she never took off the stars glimmered to no end.

"Thank you, Marina," he muttered, returning his sight to the stars. "Thank you for everything."

"Twas my pleasure, Captain. At least I kept thee sober for some time."

She remained quiet whilst he laughed but resumed her thoughts aloud, almost fearfully. "Thou knowest I must leave thee soon." Arnav did not speak for a second, struggling to fathom her unpleasant words, and swallowed. "I don't want you to go, Marina."

"I know."

The mermaid leaned over on her side to face the merchant captain, who seemed heartbroken and refused to look at her. "I do not understand, Marina," he spoke, sitting up. "I do not understand any of this. If it is true, you came here to help me… If it is true, you came here to renew the spirits of an unhappy man of the sea, then stay."

"I shall never leave thee, Captain. Not really. I swear it."

"Won't I ever see you again?"

"Aye," she smiled, using his form of speech, and glancing away. "Someday."

Again, he steadily mumbled, "I do not want you to go…" and took her hand. "I have never had anyone in life that stayed. For the most part, because I failed to save many of them from disaster."

Compassionately Marina resumed her resolve.

"I shall say this onto thee plainly, Connor Arnav, forgive thyself and forgive those who were so cruel to thee."

Seeing his impatience to disagree, she spoke faster.

"Forgive thy parents for abandoning thee as I once forgave mine. Forgive the injustices done against thee by soulless monsters like Fox. Men, such as he, have sealed their own fates without thy help and are so unworthy of thy cares. And blame thyself no more for the loss of those dearly loved."

"You ask me to do the impossible, Marina."

"That hast ne'er been a problem for thee before."

Now, our merchant captain fell silent.

"Many a time and oft thee pled for guidance and waited patiently to receive it. Well, know this. Thou canst be happy and hateful all at once. Never surrender thy quest for justice, Captain but know that it will not be found at the bottom of a bottle, and there is no one left to reap vengeance upon other than thyself, which is wrong."

"I do not know what you mean, Marina," Arnav's sights fell into his palm. "All I know is that I love you, and I do not want you to leave me. I greatly fear my future without you."

"I do not believe that" was her calm reply with a hand upon his solemn face. "Thou hast never truly feared anything for years because of courage. Courage forged and strengthened by so much hardship."

Accepting her words, he bobbed his head, finding it difficult to be depressed after such a day.

"Venture henceforth into the perilous seas and leave all thy worries, cares, and fears on the docks where they belong. Thy true destiny lies at sea, and there one day, ye will find me again. Fair winds may they always come unto thee, Captain Connor Arnav."

Slumber fell upon Arnav, but it did not come without a fight. Closely, he held the mermaid's hand in his knowing that she would soon be gone. "I shall never forget you, Marina," he murmured, drifting off. "Never."

The sun stood in the same place it had been when their journey began the previous day, and he left to contemplate whether it was all real or not. Arnav stood by the surf, now dressed in fresh, clean clothes, and wondering if everything he experienced was only a dream. True, he awoke on the beach, fatigued with his clothes in shreds. True, his limbs so sore they swung heavily as chains. Sure, there were recollections of stunning sights - swimming with dolphins, whales, and exploring sunken shark-infested galleons; of miracles such as breathing underwater, but he wouldn't dare to try such a thing as that again.

Memories of that beautiful young stowaway girl returning from the dead as a mermaid and he accountable for her demise. "Remembrances formed in a prodigious visitation," he felt though sorely unsatisfied. "My sense of guilt and subconscious contriving to concoct such a delightful fantasy. Perhaps my loneliness played a part."

The inlet shined bright, scattered with fishermen. The locals seemed to believe that the sun had finally returned to linger in St. Augustine for a spell, and our merchant captain concurred. Arnav spent that morning playing fetch with Hector and never took his eyes off the sea.

Even when throwing a piece of driftwood for the dog, his every gaze drifted towards the blue. He felt that he would always be searching for Marina, everywhere and upon every wave. He felt that for the rest of his days, he'd always mistake a slight ripple in the surf for her and any singular disturbance adrift upon the open ocean for her.

That any time he'd set up a line to hook a fish, he'd be careful not to pierce her lip. A time or two, he walked into the water at a knee's length and cried out Marina's name in vain. Woefully, there never came an answer.

He needed to repair the dinghy but couldn't rouse himself. Only the thought of how ghastly his appearance must have been stirred him despite being fully dressed.

His beard had gone untrimmed and his hair uncombed for days, but luckily when your only family member is a dog, they do not seem to mind.

"I must look as motley as you do," he declared, staring down at his pet with pure devotion.

"Come on, let's go shave a bit. You could use a good shearing too, you know."

An infant palm grew by the porch of his boathouse lonesome, and there the frayed clothes lay drying on the trunk. Our merchant captain thought for some time, feeling compelled to examine and salvage them somehow.

Standing there, he had the idea to use them as rags and perhaps fold a bandana or two for Hector.

He threw the shirt over one arm but lifted the trousers only to find them weighted down. "What in blazes?"

For a moment, he stood dumbstruck after dropping the article of clothing in the sand out of anxious hope.

"No, no, it can't be."

With a shaking hand, he kneeled over and searched one pocket to find it empty but felt the circular outline in the other. "Nay, nay it cannot be," thought he again and remembered the ghostly galleon.

Arnav delayed and rubbed his fingers together, not ready for the disappointment sure to come. Hector watched over him now, curious as to what his master was looking for.

The gold escudo coin burned bright when he slowly removed it from the pocket and into the sun. The crusader's cross had been laid in so deep that Arnav's mouth fell wide open at the sight of it. Its dark yellowish shade defined every immaculate, royal detail fashioned on both sides.

He marveled at the perfect state his pocket-sized piece of treasure was in and ran on the beach shouting and screaming with joy. The dog hadn't an idea why his master rejoiced but felt excited too and ran about him barking.

Happily, he clutched the doubloon and fell upon his knees in the surf, looking to the skies with hope again.

"I shall undertake more voyages," Arnav proclaimed while gleefully tackling the dog in gentle currents. "We shall go together, Hector, you and me! I shall return to the merchant service. We'll brave tempests and maelstroms and cannibals and roll across the entire world on a rusted tub! How exciting an adventure this will be! Every taste of life we'll savor like fine wine!"

Then, with a certain dismay, he began to think about his home and stroked his beard in consideration. He never failed to be appreciative for this rusted old shack after all the nights it provided him shelter.

"Of course, we shan't go right away," he spoke, smiling and fondly thinking on friends in the tavern. "But once we do, we will always return here to the place that made us so glad, Hector."

Again, Captain Connor Arnav admired the gold in the palm of his hand and felt the minted indentations with the other. He then gazed longingly over the horizon, feeling both giddy, and once again, envious at dolphins leaping past the inlet pondering how a salvaged coin could give salvation - no feasible explanation other than the divine.

"Forever, I will wear this coin round my neck and yearn for the day to be reunited with Marina so that we may leap amongst the dolphins again!"

THE END

"To all ye weary travelers across the seas. Fair winds may they always come unto thee…"

- *Summer Rose Peck*

Made in the USA
Columbia, SC
27 April 2022